(Leap)

(Leap)

jane breskin zalben

Alfred A. Knopf — New York

www.randomhouse.com/kids

Educators and librarians, for a variety of teaching tools, visit us at
www.randomhouse.com/teachers

Library of Congress Cataloging-in-Publication Data
Zalben, Jane Breskin.
Leap / Jane Breskin Zalben. — 1st ed.
p. cm.
SUMMARY: In the midst of the usual teenage angst over romantic relationships and figuring out their place in the world, childhood friends Krista and Daniel reconnect when, in the sixth grade, Daniel is temporarily paralyzed.
ISBN 978-0-375-83871-2 (trade) — ISBN 978-0-375-93871-9 (lib. bdg.)
[1. Identity—Fiction.   2. Paralysis—Fiction.   3. People with disabilities—Fiction.   4. Rehabilitation—Fiction.   5. Friendship—Fiction.
6. Swimming—Fiction.   7. Queens (New York, N.Y.)—Fiction.]   I. Title.
PZ7.Z254Lb 2007
[Fic]—dc22   2006016076

Printed in the United States of America
January 2007
10 9 8 7 6 5 4 3 2 1
First Edition

To Jonathan and Alexander—

With each step you take in your journeys,

my heart is filled

with uncertainty and joy

leap (leep) *v:* to spring, jump, rise, bound, transition

leap and the net will appear
(Zen saying)

"A friend owes kindness to one in despair."
—Job 6:14

One

Krista

There's a crack in everything.
That's how the light gets in.
—from "Anthem," by Leonard Cohen, songwriter

The best part about living on Twenty-fifth Avenue in Flushing, Queens, is that Bobby Kaufman is three blocks away on Twenty-seventh. Three blocks, not two, because there is also Twenty-fifth Road, then Twenty-sixth Avenue and Twenty-seventh. By some wonderful fluke of nature, Twenty-seventh Avenue is where the cutest boys from P.S. 79 ended up. About a half a dozen girls around my age—twelve—live on mine, including Elana Michaels. Everyone calls her Lainie. She wears fluffy vintage angora sweaters from the sixties that she found in thrift stores in the East Village, pretends that the rhinestone heart around her neck is real diamonds, and has been modeling since she was in diapers. The fancy photograph of her face hanging over the white upright piano in her living room—a piano that is rarely played—is called a "head shot." Only her first name, Elana, and her agent's phone number are on the bottom. (Her agent is really her mother.) Nobody in their right mind needs a Lainie living on their block.

My two best friends since the fourth grade are Sandy Doyle and Gina Deluca. Sandy and I ride our bikes every weekend. We pick up Gina along the way and head toward Twenty-seventh Avenue, which we call "the block." Going there is more exciting than going to any other part of the neighborhood, even Carmine's Ices, where Gina's uncle gives us free samples of Lemon Zest and Tutti Frutti.

Just as we get to the beginning of the block, my head and chest begin to throb, half hoping the boys will be outside, the other half praying they're not. I always do this Zen thing—take a deep breath and say to myself, *Krista Harris, stay cool*—but it never works. If we see any of them, instead of slowing down we pedal faster. What if one of them waved? Or actually talked to us? Still, that doesn't stop us from going over there. Pretending we don't notice them has become a game.

In the second half of third grade, Bobby K. noticed me. Well, maybe. On Valentine's Day, when I came back from recess, a giant heart-shaped box of chocolates was on my chair. Bobby didn't actually hand it to me. He stood off to the side, smiling, as if he had a secret. So how could I be 100 percent sure? It had the name *Kaufman's Fine Handmade Chocolates* glimmering in gold script across the red silk lid. Bobby Kaufman's grandfather owns a candy store on Northern Boulevard where he hand-dips chocolates as well as fruit, nuts, and almost anything else edible that doesn't squirm. He'd probably hand-dip my little brother, Matt, if he stayed in one spot long enough.

Matt and I went through the entire two layers, biting most of them in half and putting the uneaten halves back in their little silver foil cups. We fought over the last mocha marshmallow covered in bittersweet chocolate, but I got it and didn't split it with him. Matt was stuck with the cherry cordial, syrup oozing down his chubby chin. Even he knew at age four that kind was as disgusting as marzipan. And I knew that Bobby was as smooth as that creamy mocha one.

I saved the candy box, lining it with scrap fabric left over from a quilt my mother had been making. In it I put all my jewelry, my grandfather's engraved pocket watch Grandma had given me after he died, and the precious note I had found hidden under the candy box lid. It was an unsigned valentine written on a piece of paper ripped from a notebook, part of a math problem scribbled at the top, folded into a small square. On a single blue line in the center, written in pencil, was one sentence: *Do you love me?* Next to the question were two tiny boxes. I added an *x* in the yes box. Was it Bobby's handwriting? We had just learned script. What if it wasn't? What if it was Harry Peters, who wore his retainer in school with neon rubber bands on his front teeth, slurping his *s*'s? And anyone who sat next to him needed heavy-duty rain gear good enough for the Amazon rain forest. Or worse,

Jeremy Wainraff, who smelled like blue cheese from the lotion he applied on his dry, reptilian skin. I kept the note in the candy box where I found it, the answer unde-livered, so I never discovered for sure who my true secret admirer really was. If it turns out to be Bobby, I will die. I never told anyone. Not even Sandy or Gina. And I tell them *everything*.

Now, two and a half years later, I still have this big crush on Bobby that I can't make go away no matter how hard I try, and trust me, I've tried. Big-time. If Daniel and I were still close, I might have stuffed the note in his face. I'd have asked, "Is this from your best friend?" But I can't.

Since Daniel and I stopped being friends, there are images of him I can't get out of my head. *Daniel is sitting next to me in the sandbox on our first day of kindergarten. Some-one spills sand on me and I begin to cry. Daniel leans over, flicks the grains away from my eyelids with his finger, finds a used tis-sue in the pocket of his overalls, and wipes the tears streaming down my cheeks. I'm impressed even at five years old. So we be-come inseparable. We eat lunch together. Have play dates. Pick each other for teams.* By fourth grade, though, the boys began to tease him about his best friend being a girl. And the last thing Daniel wanted was to be called a sissy.

They shouted in the schoolyard, "Are you getting any? Is she your girlfriend?"

At the bus stop they poked each other in the side. "Do you do it?" I didn't think they even knew what "it" was.

So when Coach told Daniel in gym, "Pick someone to be on your soccer team," and Daniel walked straight past me—like I didn't even exist, as if I were a bug to be flung off someone's arm—and said, "Bobby," simply because he was a boy, that was the beginning of our end. I cried myself to sleep that night. Who would I take turns with buying the next number in the mystery series we had been collecting? Match backpacks with each fall? Who would be my swim buddy at the pool club under the Whitestone Bridge? Who would be honest enough to tell me when my breath smelled like a dog? Or that I had a poppy seed from a bagel stuck in a front tooth?

The final picture I have in my mind of Daniel is a few weeks before fifth-grade graduation. *It's three o'clock. He's surrounded by friends. His long black hair—silken as a raven's wing—tosses in front of his eyes as he zooms past Jack's Stationery Store on his skateboard. Daniel's whirling, wearing his iPod. The sun is shining. Blazing on the pavement.*

The next day there were the phone calls, parents trying to find out details as the news spread. With more and more calls, the story got gorier and changed from call to call.

What happened? Is it true? Is Daniel going to be okay?

My mother cried after she found out. At the dinner table. Stacking the dishes in the dishwasher. Staring out the window as she tried to draw or paint or sew.

That night as I lay in bed pretending to be asleep, I overheard my parents talking.

"He's so talented. And bright. He had everything going for him."

Well, he still does, doesn't he? It's not like Daniel's dead or something.

A few minutes later Mom tiptoed into my room, waiting to hear me breathe like she did when I was little. Finally I said, "Ma, it's not like it happened to me or Matt."

"I know," she sobbed as she sat down on the edge of my bed. A soaked handkerchief was balled up in the palm of her hand. "A single moment, and a person's whole life can turn around."

She held me and wouldn't let go. That was when I felt her fear. For me, not Daniel.

And I knew I had to do something.

Top Ten List

1. Help Daniel
(without taking sides and pissing Bobby off).
2. Discover who gave me the love note—this century.
3. Find out who Bobby likes.
(Keep your fingers crossed!)
4. Try to stop the B obsession
(see numbers 1 through 3).
5. Learn to be a nicer person.
(Lain rhymes with pain.)
6. Lose at least five pounds.
(Even though the magazines claim #9, they say how to do #6.)
7. Kiss a boy on the lips.
(Spin the Bottle at camp doesn't count.)
8. Find out what I want most in life. Who am I?
(Simple question? Not!)
9. Accept what is.
(Yeah, right. Who came up with that big idea?)
10. Delete #9. Change.
(Easier said than done.)

Two

Daniel

Life is what happens to you while
you're busy making other plans.
—John Lennon, musician

You know how life goes along and you don't always stop
to think, *Is it okay?* You're just too busy doing everyday
stuff: homework, hanging out, watching TV, going to the
movies. Well, life caused me to grow up fast. Real fast.
Like overnight.

Almost everyone I knew was heading for sleepaway
camp the weekend of July 4. We had long "graduated"
from Y day camps and the pool club where Krista and I
had been buddies in the Barracudas growing up. Bobby
was going off to train with some hotshot coach. A lot of
the girls were going to Girl Scout camp somewhere in
upstate New York for a couple of weeks. Their trunks
were probably packed, like ours, and sent.

A month before, my mother had taken me for a camp
physical. I also had a routine dental exam. An X-ray
picked up by our family dentist showed there was an

extra tooth in the roof of my mouth, called an odon-toma. One little tooth under the skin that no one could even see. A tooth so tiny, the Tooth Fairy would pass it up.

"My dad yanks out things like that all the time in his office. Or you could go to the aquarium. Don't sharks have multiple rows of teeth?" Bobby had teased.

When we went in for a consultation, Dr. Robert Kaufman, oral surgeon, told my parents, "Simple operation. With general anesthesia. He'll be sedated with an IV in his arm. Like a deep sleep." Then he turned to me, smiling, "When you wake up, you'll feel some discomfort, but you'll be off and running in no time. No big deal."

But it was a big deal. I had a bad allergic reaction while I was put out. My lungs started filling up with mucus like I was having an asthma attack. They said my throat closed up so I couldn't breathe and the bronchial spasms got worse and worse. And wouldn't stop. The spot where they took the tooth out started bleeding, like in one of those horror movies—spurting blood all over the place. I started choking. No one had ever heard of such a thing in an office visit for removing a measly baby tooth. Until now. They rushed me by ambulance to the emergency room at the hospital. I don't remember a thing. The dictionary says that an accident is a misfortune that happens "unintentionally." Tell *that* to my parents.

When I opened my eyes and saw a bright white light I thought, *This is it. I'm dead.* Then I felt this tube snaking down my throat and it hurt something awful. My mother put wet cotton gauze on my dry, cracked lips and had me suck on it—doing her pushy mother thing, so I knew I was alive. She kissed my forehead, grabbed my hand, and then telephoned my father, "He's waking up. You've got to leave court, now. The doctors say there might be some oxygen loss to his brain. Please hurry."

Dad raced over to the hospital faster than Superman.

I heard my mom saying, "He needs a transfusion. I'm not his blood type."

While Dad gave some of his, my mother called all the people she imagined had "safe" blood. Then she said to my father as she stood wrapped in his arms, looking at me, "What's safe anymore?"

Krista's mom took off from teaching and rushed over to donate blood as soon as she heard we were both A positive. My mother and Krista's hugged, without saying a thing, and stayed like that for several moments. We had been studying the body in school the week it happened, and I thought, *Her corpuscles will flow through my veins. We'll be linked.* I liked that. I missed not having Krista as my best friend, and if I was connected to her mother, then in a way wasn't Krista connected to me too?

The whole class chipped in and sent a stuffed bear holding a bouquet of balloons when I was transferred to the rehab wing of the hospital. The note attached to its ear said: *We all miss you, buddy. Get well soon, or else. Your old class, 5A.* Even Bobby signed it.

"It must have been rough on him. With his father and all. It's not like it was his fault. It wasn't anyone's," I said once I could talk in full sentences.

"Rough on *him*?" My mother glared at me as if I had completely lost my mind. "What about *you*?" She stroked my leg, where I had no feeling.

Greeting cards lined the walls of my hospital room. No matter how hard everyone tried to make me feel like it was home, it was what it was: a place of rehabilitation, where I'd have to learn things all over again from the beginning—like walking. I felt like a baby as my mother helped me get to the bathroom. And at almost twelve, that really sucked.

At the beginning, Krista's father visited me every day. Not because he was so friendly or had nothing else to do, but because Mr. Harris had become my physical therapist. My mother had used him years ago, when she practiced too much—especially the Kreisler cadenzas in the Beethoven violin concerto she had been rehearsing for a chamber music recital. He helped her wrists and shoulders release tension. When those nervous twitches started coming back, my father said to her, "Maybe you need him as much as Daniel does now."

She glanced up at my father. "I'll be okay. We need to be here for Daniel." Later, when she thought I was asleep, she put her head into her hands, her voice choking. "My beautiful Daniel."

On our first visit, she started giving Mr. Harris the

third degree. "When do you expect him to sit up on his own? I trust your word over those doctors," she told him, wanting more, as if he had all the answers.

"Hey, didn't I do that around five months old?" I broke in. "You called me precocious."

Mr. Harris looked at me thoughtfully, smiled, and then turned his gaze to my mother. "Soon, I hope."

"That's great." Dad tried to sound upbeat. "Isn't that great, Emma?"

My mother paused, looking like she was trying to remain together and calm, like she did before one of her concerts. "His legs? When can he use them?"

"He will, Mrs. Rosen. Emma." Mr. Harris looked into her eyes. "These things take time."

Dad put his arm around Mom. She tensed her fingers into a fist and pulled away like she did when they had a fight over something stupid. "How long?" she continued, her lips pursed into a thin line.

I tried to wiggle my toes under the sheet, to show everybody I was okay, but I couldn't feel them. *Yeah, how long?* I wanted to scream. *What do you mean, these things take time?*

"You know, he's a swimmer," she rambled on.

"Everyone knows that, Emma," replied Mr. Harris. "All those races written up."

"I've been taking him to the Y since he was four." She grinned in my direction, remembering, but through the smile I saw a sadness in her eyes. "Daniel's dream is to be in the Olympics. Every day we'd get up at five-thirty and go for laps."

Mr. Harris looked past my mother to my father. For help? Dad bit his lower lip.

When Coach showed up during the summer, he pushed down the metal bar that held the mattress like a crib, and patted my legs. I had trouble feeling them. "Now you'll have to work hard at walking instead of swimming. It's not going to be easy, but you already know about sacrificing for what you want, don't you?"

For me, it was being able to have that quiet rush in my head, with my only focus skimming the water and winning. "It's a different kind of winning this time, isn't it?"

"Sometimes when you lose something, it's possible to gain something else. Life can surprise you. Look at this as an opportunity," he said.

"How could *this* be an opportunity?" I was terrified.

So was Mom. But she tried not to show it. She sat by my side on the edge of the bed, on top of the Moroccan throw she'd brought in, and carefully cut stars out of metallic paper, mounting them on the hospital ceiling, forming more constellations each day. At night, they glowed in the dark, reminding me of when I was little and she'd plugged my night-light in the outlet by the baseboard molding so I wouldn't be scared. She lay down next to me on the pillow and sometimes put on music. Other times, silence took us somewhere else. Away from fluorescent bulbs in sterile corridors. Away from nurses' voices over the intercom calling for doctors or announcing that visiting hours were over. Away from the pain of remembering as we tried to return to before. When things were normal.

The day I left the hospital with my parents, I looked over at my father filling out release forms. He seemed very tired. He had buttoned his shirt unevenly, off by one hole. A nurse's aide guided me in a wheelchair to the curb. Mom was parked with our car by the entrance, gleeful that I was finally leaving. Dad kissed the top of my head as they lifted me onto the seat. I leaned on him for support, and he whispered, "Come on, Dan, it's time to go home." Home was going to be a foreign place after being in rehab for the entire summer. Could I handle it?

I don't know who stopped being friends first—me or Bobby. Because of how the accident happened. We just didn't talk afterward. And he never came to visit. Half of me understood. Some people get freaked out by hospitals, especially when everyone thinks that person's parent might have caused the stay. But the other half of me thought, *How could he not have come to see me?* Even though I wished he had had the courage, I still missed being with the group on Twenty-seventh Avenue—dribbling basketballs on one of their driveways, playing catch, walking Max, Bobby's golden retriever, with him after school. And then there were the swim meets at the Y and at other places, where Bobby and I were on the same team, but at the same time always competing against each other. We'd take turns who would come in first. All that was over.

The beginning of sixth grade was a wash. Everyone was starting middle school. Well, everyone except me. I bet Bobby had a new pair of high-tops, while I was gliding a walker around my house like an old man, wearing white crew socks and sweats. Mom decided to take time off from everything—practicing her violin, giving music lessons—to home-school me. It was like she was going back to the time when she'd taken care of her younger sister, my aunt Edna—they were sixteen years apart—when their mama got sick and died.

The first day she was rougher than my teachers. She drilled me in math. We did grammar. Began Latin. And it wasn't like I could run around with my friends during recess to blow off steam. The second day she tried to teach me about physics. We made paper planes and flew them around the room to demonstrate Bernoulli's principle. One zoomed out the window into a neighbor's plastic baby pool. We laughed until our stomachs ached at the squeals of the toddler watching it tumble outside. On the third day, she read to me, even from the Bible— and I'd always thought jazz was Mom's religion. I hoped she wasn't getting all weird on me like those born-again types. Ribbons of light, like out of a movie, streamed through my bedroom window, hitting the Scripture on her lap. It was eerie. She sighed and glanced up. " 'When the morning stars sang together, all divine beings shouted for joy.' It's poetry. From the Book of Job. That's some story. God made Job suffer. He wasn't a bad man. Should good people suffer?"

I shook my head. Did I deserve this? A twelve-year-old boy stuck with his mother, listening to her quote the Bible like one of those holy rollers?

"Maybe to test him?" Mom continued her one-sided conversation.

Oh, so God is testing me? Nice, Ma, real nice. Now it's my *fault?*

"God took away everything from him: his home, his fortune, his family, his health."

"That's not fair," I said.

"Who said life's fair? Maybe we shouldn't expect it to be." She drew me closer, leaning her head on my shoulder. "At one time or another, maybe we're all being tested."

"Maybe." I rested my head on hers. "But what do we have to do to pass?"

She sucked in her breath, exhaled, and looked into my eyes.

"Hey, I've got a warm place to sleep. I've got you, Dad, unlimited pizza, and DVDs, so I figure I'm way ahead of the game," I said.

She squeezed me. "We'll get through this together. I promise you, Daniel." Then she hugged me harder than she ever had. And I believed her.

Mom tried with all her heart to remain optimistic—and she did, until the cards stopped coming, the balloons lost their air and bobbed limply on the floor, and friends returned to school and after-school activities. Then she got quieter and quieter. The house felt empty until Dad got home from work. Some days I didn't hear a sound other than my own breath while I studied or the low hum of her computer as she searched for some quick cure.

I missed seeing everyone's faces during the day. Especially Coach, Coach, Cockroach, who had transferred to the middle school. There was one face I did see, and that was Krista's. I had to go to physical therapy three times a week at her dad's office, which was in the large converted basement of their home. And that's when I hoped things might change.

Three

Krista

Try brushing your teeth tonight with your other hand.
—Ken Burns, documentary filmmaker

When Daniel didn't start school in September, the gossip began. *Did you hear about Daniel?* It went around the schoolyard like wildfire. *Can he walk? Is he coming back to school?* Our new school. Would Daniel still be Daniel? The friend in the sandbox. The person who swam more laps than everyone else in the neighborhood, even Bobby.

"He no longer looks like himself," Lainie reported at lunch. Whatever popped into her head came out of her mouth.

Gina scowled. "How do *you* know what he looks like?"

"Have you seen him?" Sandy piped up with curiosity, licking cream off her third Oreo.

"I heard," Lainie said, shrugging. "Things."

Gina rolled her eyes at Sandy and me in disbelief.

"My mother said Bobby's father will be lucky to yank out a dog's tooth," Lainie continued, pulling on the gold stud next to a tiny ruby one in her pierced ear.

"It wasn't on purpose," I protested.

"Makes no difference. Bet the Kaufmans move. Too bad. Bobby is so-o-o, so adorable." Lainie curled a newly highlighted strand of hair around her manicured index finger.

I ran home, took the old love note from my heart-shaped candy box, unfolded the square, and smoothed the creases of the crinkled paper out on my bedspread.

Please, please, let him stay.

My prayers were answered. The Kaufmans didn't move.

After so many years, why did I still think Bobby was wonderful? He wasn't perfect. That's for sure. I had heard through my father that he didn't visit Daniel in the hospital. But how could he? People blamed Dr. Kaufman. Was it Bobby's fault what his father had done? Bobby had collected money to send the bear and balloons to the hospital, hadn't he? I felt caught between whose side to take, Daniel's or Bobby's, which was dumb because this wasn't about taking sides. Why did I have to choose because *they* didn't talk? Still, I couldn't make the feeling go away.

As weeks went by, my father reported at the dinner table about Daniel's slow, steady improvement. "Daniel brushed his teeth and combed his hair today. He had real food. Clear broth. He's working his way up to Jell-O and applesauce. He's making big strides."

Was Dad for real? Daniel loved to ride his bike to Carmine's or the pizza place for a slice after school. Now that was *real* food. I had read in the newspaper that if you were on a desert island and pizza was your only source of food, you could survive on it for years. Daniel was a survivor, but not on Jell-O. Not the Daniel I knew. I made up my mind that when he returned to school I'd throw him a pizza party. I'd get a pizza with everything on it—the works: meatballs, mushrooms, and extra mozzarella.

I confided to Gina, "I wouldn't trade places with him for anything in the world, but there's another part of me that envies Daniel."

"Envies?" Gina was aghast.

"He doesn't have to straighten his room, do homework, or babysit an obnoxious brother."

"Let's face it," Gina replied, "when you have trouble going to the bathroom by yourself, doing a book report on Ponce de Leon doesn't seem like such a big deal anymore."

I wanted to take back what I had said.

When Daniel was released from the hospital, he started coming to my father's private office in our house, where Dad saw patients outside of rehab. One day, I peeked from behind the curtains of my bedroom window to get a glimpse of him coming up the path—to see with my own eyes that he was okay. Well, I knew he wasn't okay. But I didn't believe he was as bad as some people, like Lainie, made out. At the same time I was afraid to look, afraid of what I'd see. *Please be okay, Daniel.*

What I saw was Daniel's mother guiding a shrunken Daniel, his hair cropped short, no longer touching the edge of his chin, and his shoulders slumped, steering a metal contraption up the ramp. My legs trembled. I broke into a sweat and my stomach ached. He looked up, caught a glimpse of me spying behind the curtains, and gave a weak, defeated smile. I waved and quickly backed away. What had I expected? I wished I could make bad things disappear with a stroke of the magic wand that Matt kept in the toy chest at the foot of his bed. I went into the bathroom and threw up in the toilet bowl.

When Sandy and Gina IM'd me later that night, I told them I had seen him.

Sandy wrote, "How does he look?"

Gina wanted to know, "Is he okay?"

They both called when I didn't IM back.

I lied and said, "Fine," because I couldn't speak over the lump lodged in my throat. Then I lit a lavender-scented candle, spilled bath crystals in the bathtub, and got in with a new paperback—one of my favorite things to do. The words on the page blurred as tears dripped onto my chest, mixing with the water. What would it feel like to be helpless? What if I could no longer read in the tub, or get out when I wanted? Would I rather be off this earth? Did Daniel feel that way when he opened his eyes each morning? Did he dream of the old Daniel like I did? The Daniel who did 360's on his skateboard on the sloped cement path behind the supermarket?

I stepped out of the water—a simple act he could no longer do unassisted—and nearly slipped, but caught myself, holding on to the ceramic soap dish attached to the tiled wall. *I'm never looking out the window for Daniel again.*

It worked for a few months, until Dad said it was time for Daniel to go back to school, and the mean me could no longer pretend he didn't exist. The real me—the one who knew I hadn't done the right thing, who should have treated Daniel the way I'd want to be treated—was angry at the other, selfish me. I just didn't want to lose Bobby—in case there was anything remotely to lose—by taking sides with Daniel.

I thought that when it comes down to it, there are guys—not many on the face of the planet—who look like rock stars. They wear bleached jeans and thin, twine-colored ropes on their wrists, or whatever style is in that month. They seem moody and complicated and cool and distant. They play loud music. Form garage bands. Strum electric guitars, never acoustic. That's Bobby. Then there are the sweet guys. They can be cute too, but in a different way—like puppies to be cuddled. They can also be well liked and popular, like Daniel. But when it comes down to it, it's the edgy guy who really does it for you. He's the coffee almond swirl ice cream, and you're willing to risk the nuts even if you're allergic. Not that I thought Daniel was plain vanilla. He had chips. But he didn't have the swirls. It's the Bobbys who make your stomach do flips, your heart race faster than a triathlon, and your body feel like you have a 104-degree fever. Right?

Four

Daniel

Hope is the thing with feathers
that perches in the soul and sings the tune without the words
and never stops at all.
—Emily Dickinson, poet

My mother insisted, "I'm driving you. It's your first day back."

"No, you're not!" I shouted. "No one's seeing my mother drive me to school. It's lame!" Bad choice of words. "Da-a-d," I groaned as I tossed my lunch into my backpack.

She threw her car keys on the kitchen countertop. "Bruce, talk some sense into him, please!"

"He'll be okay," Dad assured Mom, rubbing her back. I think she didn't want me to see the tears in her eyes as she wiped her face with a corner of the dishtowel.

A horn beeped out front. I saw a van painted school bus yellow with a hand-lettered sign hanging low on the side window: SPECIAL NEEDS VAN. I zipped up my backpack. "Okay, I'm out of here."

My mother tried to put on a good face, to not look frightened.

"See you later, alligators."

Dad gave me a playful pat on the back, the way he did before a race. "Good luck."

I wheeled my walker over to my mother to say goodbye. "Ma?"

She swallowed hard and edged a smile.

"Come on, Ma. I'll be fine in the van."

Still facing the sink, she let out a deep sigh, but I could see her eyes were red and swollen when she turned around. Then she said softly, "Wait a sec. In case you get hungry later." Her hand was shaking as she handed me a granola bar. She kissed the top of my head, inhaled, and whispered into my hair, "I love you, Daniel. Take care of yourself."

"Don't worry, I'll be okay. Really."

I said it as bravely as I could, trying to put any doubt out of my mind.

She walked me to the curb, not able to hold herself back from seeing me off, and forced a cheerful smile and waved as we drove away.

As the van pulled into the school parking lot next to the other buses, I prayed none of my friends would see me getting off. Had I become one of those people you don't want to stare at but you kind of look at from the corner of your eye, and wonder: *How does that person get dressed in the morning? Comb their hair? Brush their teeth? Live?*

When the steel lift of the van leveled with the sidewalk, the driver turned to me as he prepared to aid some other children who were a lot worse off. "Need any help, kid?"

"No thanks."

My prayers weren't answered. My regular neighborhood bus was unloading at the exact same moment as the van. Bobby piled out of the bus with a bunch of other boys from Twenty-seventh Avenue. Our eyes locked. I couldn't tell who was more uncomfortable, him or me. I headed toward the back entrance with everyone else, acting as if it were any other regular school day—not my first since school started two months ago. When he went past me, he mumbled under his breath, "Glad you're back."

"Thanks." I smiled, looking down as he rushed toward the brick school building.

Lainie eased in line next to me. "Danny boy, how's it going? You look great." Was she lying? She tapped my walker. "My grandma had one of those after a hip replacement."

Thanks a lot, Lainie. All I said was, "Oh," as one of the wheels twirled in a crack in the asphalt. My legs wobbled like a newborn colt's as I tried to push the walker forward. I was forcing it with all my might when I noticed Krista coming off the bus with her other friends. She paused when she saw me. For a moment, our eyes met. Then her gaze turned to Lainie, who was racing up the stairs two steps at a time to catch up with Bobby. I watched Krista watching them, pretending that I was searching for something in my pockets.

Krista got flustered as she passed me. "Welcome back, Daniel," she faltered. I followed her, but she forgot to hold open the door as we went in, and it slammed on my walker, halfway inside the entryway. "Oh, Daniel, Daniel, I'm so sorry." Krista rushed to my side but continued to look over her shoulder, searching. Searching for whom? Lainie? Bobby?

"Trying to get rid of me my first day back? Nice try," I joked, trying to keep it light.

A teacher's aide barreled her way over. "Be more careful, young lady!" she scolded as Krista and some other students scrambled to gather my scattered things, putting them back in the wire basket attached to the front of my walker.

"I'm so sorry," she apologized again. "Hope I didn't squash your lunch."

"Just me," I teased. "Semi-squashed. I was already halfway in."

"Truce?" we said at the same time, adding, "Jinx," smiling like old times.

Krista asked sheepishly, "You'll be okay? Homerooms are now on the second floor."

I nodded. She walked me to the elevator next to the main office, which had the words BLEEKER MIDDLE SCHOOL etched in shiny brass over the doorway. I went up with two teachers I didn't know and thought of the year Bobby broke his leg in elementary school. He got a hall pass to ride up and down whenever he pleased. Everyone thought it was soooo cool then. It didn't feel cool now. I didn't have signatures and hearts in colored marker wishing me good luck all over a tattered, weather-beaten cast.

The class was already seated when I came into home-room. Mr. James, our team teacher, saw me and grinned. Thank God he didn't make a big deal out of it. He had visited me a couple of weeks before I officially started school again, handing me his cell number and saying to me, "If you need anything, I'm a phone call away. It will all work out. You'll see." I'd just looked down. How could he be so sure?

An aide led me to a desk in the back, off in a corner, where I could keep my walker out of everyone's way. She was the same one who had helped Brandon White with his reading two years ago, when his test scores dipped two grades below average. I didn't know her name—she always been just "the aide." I struggled to sit and then stand up again for the pledge, which some student re-cited over a loudspeaker. Some kids turned around, sneaking a peek at me, and it gave me a sick feeling in the pit of my stomach—like the time in second grade when the principal had made everyone stay in the audi-torium for lunchtime without a bathroom break and I peed on the floor, yellow liquid trickling down the rows like a stream to the foot of the stage, where the principal stood at the mike. By the afternoon somehow word got around, and everyone knew it was me. My mother brought clean underwear and pants to the office. She thought she had saved me, but what I really wanted her to do was to tell that principal off for being such a jerk, so I could go home with her instead of returning to class. Sort of like today.

When the morning announcements were over, Mr. James, who was also our science teacher, held up an old newspaper article. "A new species of animal, *Symbion pandora,* was discovered in 1995. It's the size of a pinpoint and eats leftover food that spills from a lobster's mouth. Their relationship is *symbiotic.* Can anyone tell me what that word means?"

"Like Brandon and Bobby," Gina murmured.

So now they're inseparable, like we used to be?

Lainie raised her hand. "Do lobsters even have lips to spill food?"

"Hey, lobster lips, you melt me like butter." Brandon looked Lainie up and down. "Want to claw your way over to me?"

The entire class groaned.

"What did one clam say to another one about her shy son?" he continued.

"What?" a bunch of kids said in unison.

"Give him time, he'll come out of his shell," Brandon answered.

"And the world will be his oyster!" Bobby added.

Brandon gave him a high five, then went on. "What type of shellfish complains?"

"A crab!" a bunch of them yelled back at him.

Then Bobby interrupted, "What shellfish is an oxy-moron?"

"Did someone say 'moron'?" Gina muttered, looking at Brandon.

Krista ignored her and said softly, "Jumbo shrimp." Krista's face turned bright red when Bobby glanced in her direction.

After morning classes, we all headed to the cafeteria. I took the elevator down and sat at the end of our class table. Some kids glanced at my walker as they passed, looking at it like it was R2-D2. Others mumbled hi as they filed by holding hot lunch trays. My stomach grumbled, craving the pizza special instead of cold tuna fish. My mother had drawn a smiley face on the front of the brown sandwich bag, and I quickly placed a napkin on top, hoping no one had seen it. Did she think I was still in preschool? I wanted to fit in like before the accident: going on the school bus with the rest of my friends, taking two steps at a time on the stairwell, waiting on line for pizza instead of having cat breath from the tuna fish. The truth was I felt left out. Even from their dumb shellfish jokes.

When I came home, my mother was at the door. "How did it go?"

"Fine."

"Really?"

"I said fine," I repeated as she poured me a glass of milk.

"Did you see Coach?"

"No," I said grudgingly. "Why would I?"

"So what did you do today?" She pushed a plate with a big cookie toward me.

"Nothing." I pushed it back even though home-baked chocolate chip was my favorite.

"Nothing?" She looked a little hurt. I was tighter than the clam in their joke.

"Okay, we learned about a species: *Symbion pandora*. Are you happy now?"

"Like in Pandora's box? It's a Greek myth. I read it to you."

I shrugged, acting like I didn't remember, or care.

My mother, full of stories, continued at full speed. "Supposedly the gods gave Pandora, the first woman, a box she must never open. Legend has it that the box was filled with all the evils of the world. Other versions say it contained blessings. Her curiosity got the better of her and she opened the box. Everything inside escaped but one."

"Yeah, so?" I said impatiently. "What was left?" I tried to hold back the day's frustrations, threatening to pour out of me like a tidal wave.

Mom popped a chunk of my chocolate-chip cookie into her mouth as the doorbell rang. It was one of her violin students, eagerly waving to her through the glass-paned back door, returning after months of canceled lessons.

"Hope," she said as she got up to let her in. "Hope."

Five

Krista

Life is a great big canvas
and you should throw
all the paint on it you can.
—*Danny Kaye, comedian and actor*

Well, I didn't give Daniel that pizza party, which should
have become number eleven on my top ten list. Or part
of number five, under learning to be a nicer person. Instead, he returned to school without a big bang.

On the way home, Gina sat next to me on the school
bus. We watched as Daniel made his way in the rain toward
the van he was going home on. He couldn't hold an umbrella and move his walker at the same time, so he looked
completely freaked out as pellets of water began to pour
down. Without realizing I was talking out loud, I yelled, "I
can't believe this! He's getting soaked!" Then I saw the
aide run after Daniel, her hooded raincoat flapping in the
wind as our bus pulled away. He seemed mad as she tried
to help him into the van. It was the same scrunched-up
face he'd had when he was seven and someone had hit

him for no reason. I let out a deep sigh, my finger tracing the raindrops hitting the outside of the window.

Gina looked in my direction. "Daniel's tough. He'll be okay."

I felt sad, remembering our first day in kindergarten together in the sandbox. Me and Daniel. Daniel and me. Then I thought of how I hadn't been there for him these last five months. "Are you trying to make me feel better, Gina?" I said, shaking my head. "Because it's not working."

Sandy said from the seat behind us, "Maybe he'll surprise us all."

"What makes you say that?" Lainie asked Sandy.

Gina twisted around. "Because Sandy always sees the glass half full." Then she mumbled to Lainie, who was sitting beside Sandy, "And you see your reflection in the whole glass."

Lainie glared at Gina and leaned back in her seat, pouting and staring at the traffic.

"She's kidding. She didn't mean it," said Sandy the optimist, trying to make peace.

I thought, *I'm always looking at the glass—half full* and *half empty. Or maybe I'm just plain looking for the glass, period.*

The four of us remained silent the rest of the way home.

When I got into the kitchen, a note was fastened to the refrigerator door under a magnet in the shape of a wrench, imprinted with Gina's father's plumbing business: "Deluca, Drain Surgeon."

Sweetie, take a snack and
come downstairs.
                    Love, Dad
P.S. Mom's picking Matt up
from school.

I tossed the note. As I was coming down the stairs, Daniel and his mother were walking up the long handicap ramp to my father's office. "Let me get that!" I held open the glass storm door as Mrs. Rosen supported him under his arms and took off his poncho. What if he'd told her what I did this morning, on his first day back at school? If I had waited for Daniel, paid attention to him, would that door have slammed on him? I felt guilty in front of his mom and prayed he kept it between us.

"Am I safe?" he asked, carefully edging his walker inside the waiting room.

"Promise," I said as the rain ran down the ramp.

"Filled your quota for ramming geeks today?" he said with a devilish grin.

"Hey, you got through your first day in one piece. You're here, aren't you?"

"Except for this girl who tried to flatten me into a tortilla," Daniel teased.

"Give it up," I said, as if the years after fourth grade had disappeared.

Mrs. Rosen seemed to be involved in taking off her raincoat and getting her umbrella folded up neatly, but if she was like my mother, she was probably pretending and hanging on our every word. Daniel smiled awkwardly, the same smile he gave when we'd sing along with tapes of Broadway show tunes that she played while she drove carpool when we were younger. She had always been my favorite mom besides my own. She had different instruments around her house that she allowed us to bang on, shouting with encouragement, "Improvise!"—never hinting we might be tone-deaf. When we built a fort from sheets and blankets in Daniel's room, she let us keep it there for at least a week or more. She'd bake healthy snacks that also tasted good—oatmeal-cranberry cookies or banana-raisin muffins. I'd watch her glass-beaded earrings dangle in the waves of her long black hair, catching sunlight like a prism. She always smelled like rosewater and spice. I wanted to be her when I grew up.

She was so unlike Lainie's mom—a control freak extraordinaire whom Gina referred to as "the Witch of Whitestone." She didn't allow Lainie to stick a poster on her wall, even with masking tape. It might ruin the decor. Lainie once put up one for two hours with pushpins and used Wite-Out to conceal the holes when she took it down before her mom came home. And God forbid a stray cookie crumb landed on the backseat of the car on the way to library story hour—we'd all be exiled to Siberia eating snow for eternity. And that's if we were lucky!

My father popped his head in the waiting room and smiled at Daniel's mother, who smiled back. Then he turned toward me and tried to kiss me on my head.

"Dad!" I ducked, wanting to crawl into a hole.

Daniel's mother and my father rolled their eyes at each other like my friends and I do.

"Honey, could you set up the last table"—he pointed—"for Daniel. My assistant couldn't come in today. Came down with the flu." He turned back to Mrs. Rosen. "Change in seasons."

She nodded. "I hate when it starts getting cold, and dark comes so much earlier. All the plants shrivel up and die. I should fly south for the winter with the birds. To somewhere full of color. Maybe visit my kid sister in Baton Rouge?" Daniel looked at her oddly. I noticed that Mrs. Rosen wasn't wearing *any* earrings. She smelled like Ben-Gay ointment from Daniel, not rosewater and spice. There were no show tunes. Just the drone of physical therapy machines in the large open space.

"Gotta go." I went over to a row of four stalls, each separated by a long cotton curtain suspended from a metal track on the ceiling. I tugged open the curtain in the empty one. A pile of used terry-cloth towels and a light blue hospital gown were on an examining table. I tossed them into a large bin in the laundry room near the garage. When I returned, I crumpled up the paper from the last patient and stretched a wide sheet of clean white paper from a thick roll across the narrow leather table where Daniel would lie down. I was happy to have the chance to make it up to Daniel for all the times I hadn't come in to just say hi.

"Ready, Dad," I called.

"Tell Daniel I'm ready to torture him."

"I heard that, Mr. H.," Daniel replied from the waiting room.

Mrs. Rosen let Daniel lean on her without the walker. He winced as he got up on the table, and his mom closed the curtain. Once he had changed into a cloth gown and was lying down, she went back to the waiting area and picked up the latest issue of *Gourmet*.

"Daniel needs hot packs on his legs today," my father said, coming over.

I walked over to a silver tub of steaming water, scooped out two packs with a pair of tongs, wrapped each one in a thick towel from the stack on top of the dryer, and handed them to my father.

"Let's get you cooked," he teased Daniel. Then Dad looked at me. "Fluff three pillows: one for Daniel's head and two for under his knees, so his back doesn't strain."

Daniel gave me a tight smile, seeming embarrassed, as I took pillows from the shelf under the examining table and put fresh pillowcases on them. "Thanks."

"No problem." I hesitated.

My father looked at me briefly as I stood there, then he grabbed the pillows, lifting Daniel's legs as he slid them comfortably underneath. As I was turning to leave, he smeared clear jelly on Daniel's legs and fastened electrodes attached to a black pocket-sized machine onto the goop glistening on the budding hairs of Daniel's thighs.

"The Blob!" Daniel made a face, pretending he was scared.

I shook my head, pulling the curtains shut behind me.

"Herr Harris," he went on in a thick Romanian accent, "keep those away from me." Suddenly he let out a blood-curdling wail as I heard my father say he was turning the machine up. I jumped, and they both cracked up.

"Very funny," I said with a smirk as my father parted the curtain with a swift sweep of his arm.

"Had you going." Daniel overheard me.

"Not for a second," I shouted over the curtain while my father went back in to check on him.

After a few minutes my father came outside and found me taking wet towels from the washing machine and throwing them into the dryer. He put his arm around me. "The machine stimulates the nerves in his muscles. Daniel only feels a slight tingle inside. Don't worry. It doesn't hurt."

I folded some clean towels. "Do I look worried?"

He tucked my hair behind my ears. I was.

When Daniel was done, he came over and sat down in the only empty chair next to me by the computer while my father and Mrs. Rosen talked in low whispers near the water cooler.

"Would you like a brownie?" I asked, closing out of my e-mail.

Daniel gave the tray the once-over. "Just one."

I handed him a brownie on a napkin with superheroes on the front, left over from Matt's sixth birthday party last year.

He took a bite and dark-brown bits of chocolate cake

circled his lips. He blushed, wiping his mouth. "I was saving them in case I got hungry later."

I took a bite and felt crumbs on my lips also. "Me too."

My father came over with Daniel's mother and kneeled down next to him, putting his hand on one of Daniel's knees. "Hey, buddy, I've got some good news for you."

"Yeah?" Daniel looked over at his mother nervously. "And what's that?"

"I was thinking you should start swimming again. It would be good therapy."

"I can't walk without this stupid thing." Daniel jabbed at the walker with his arm and it almost fell over. "How am I going to swim?"

"You know everyone's lighter in the water. There are special classes at the Y to build your strength. You'll need help at first, but trust me, it'll be good for you."

"I've seen *those* people trying to get in and out of the pool like beached whales."

"Daniel, please," Mrs. Rosen said.

"Ma." Daniel lowered his voice. "I'm not making a fool of myself in something where . . ." His voice trailed off.

"You were the best." I finished his sentence.

Daniel's eyes met mine. They were filled with tears. He quickly wiped one away with the napkin he was still holding, coated with brownie crumbs.

"*Were,*" he repeated.

His mother gently brushed his moistened cheek.

"I can't," he choked out. "I just can't."

Daniel's mother blotted his face with a tissue. "*Can't?* Oh, Daniel, that word never used to be in your vocabulary. Sweetheart, I thought you'd be happy."

She went over to the water cooler, my father following her, and got a drink.

"Daniel," I said, leaning toward him, "can't you even try? Once. See how it goes."

He shook his head.

"Wouldn't it be great if you could get back to where you were at the end of fifth grade? Before the summer." I took another brownie and offered it to him. "Come on."

"Will you help me, Krista? Just us two Barracudas."

Bobby was at the Y every afternoon like clockwork. What if he saw me with Daniel? What if anyone saw me with him doing my Clara Barton number? Then I remembered item number one on my list: help Daniel. I looked up at him, into his big brown eyes. The weight of his hope filled and scared me.

"Krista?" His voice went up slightly.

"Okay. But I can't promise a lot." I needed an out.

His face lit up. "I'll try not to let you down."

"Don't let yourself down," I said.

When Daniel and his mother left, I went upstairs. My mother was making ravioli. "Where were you?" she asked as she strained the water from the pot into the sink.

"Helping Dad out with Daniel."

"I could use some help too," she snapped. "I ran from teaching to picking up Matt to food shopping to starting dinner. Not to mention I have my *own* homework to do."

My brother ravenously sucked each plump ravioli square, making loud slurping noises as he sipped the sauce from a soup spoon. I bent down and smelled tomato and basil on his breath. "How're you doing, little tiger?" I hung his yellow rain slicker on a hook, noticing water drip from it and form puddles in the hall.

My mother watched me dab at the wooden floor with a paper towel. When I stood up, she brushed aside my bangs and kissed my forehead. "Sorry I was short with you. How is Daniel these days?"

There was a part of me that wished I could talk as casually about Daniel as my mother now could, and it made me feel low to think that, especially after this afternoon. What had I gotten myself into? A promise is a promise. I'd have to help him now. I'd just rather be *seen* with Bobby by the outside world. But I knew better. Somewhere inside of me.

Six

Daniel

Remember that as a teenager you are in the last stage of your life when you will be happy to hear that the phone is for you.
—Fran Lebowitz, satirist

Mr. James bolted into class carrying a package labeled BIOLOGICAL SUPPLIES. LIVE. DELIVER IMMEDIATELY. I glanced at the photocopied sheet on each desk. *Tadpoles are undeveloped frogs, protected from their predators by coloration, which enables them to hide, or to swim away undetected. They go from water to land in three months, depending on the temperature of the water.*

"I'm going to go from land to water. Bet that tadpole beats me by a couple of months," I whispered to Krista as we gathered in a circle around Mr. James's desk.

She gave me her stern look. "It better not."

And I thought, *It better not.*

Mr. James slid a clear plastic bag filled with watery liquid from a Styrofoam container and waved us closer. Bobby and I were eye to eye, gazing through opposite sides of the bag at two tiny eyes and a tail. We quickly glanced away from each other as the tadpole darted. Then Mr. James poured the liquid and tadpole into a large Plexiglas cube. A layer of turquoise pebbles was at the bottom, and he carefully placed a small green plastic palm tree in the corner. "Looks like this little guy's going to winter in Miami this year, minus the white Bermuda shorts," he joked. Everyone laughed. Then he continued on, reading from the brochure about how to take care of tadpoles.

"Sounds easier than walking a dog." Brandon glanced over at Bobby, and I thought of Max.

When Mr. James looked up, he said, "I'm passing around sheets on frog metamorphosis and water ecology. At the top of each handout is your name and group assignment, so you know who you will be working with. Each group in the class should carefully document what they discover—the growth, the changes, any habits this particular tadpole develops as it becomes a frog. I want to *see* your observations as budding scientists."

The good news was Krista was in my group, Group Five. The bad news: so was Bobby. And Lainie and Brandon.

Touching the tips of his fingers together, Brandon narrowed his eyes and stroked his chin. "I've gathered you all here together today to find out who amongst us is the murderer."

"Moving right along," said Bobby, taking charge and jotting down a day of the week next to each of our names. "Daniel will take Monday," he said without looking me in the eye. "Krista, Tuesday. Lainie, Wednesday, and Brandon, Thursday. So I guess I'm stuck with Friday. I thought we could make a chart recording when the tail disappears, when the gills develop, you know, stuff like that."

"Great idea," I said, glancing over.

Bobby immediately looked down.

For what felt like forever, but must have been only a split second, no one said a word.

Bobby ripped some paper from his notebook and gave each of us a slip with our name and the day of the week on it. "Okay, then," he said as the bell rang for the next period—gym, one that used to be a favorite but which I now dreaded.

Instead of going to the boys' locker room to change into shorts and a T-shirt, I went straight to the adaptive gym, separated by a folding wall inside the larger main gymnasium. Sounds of a game came from the other side. As I sat down on the bleachers, a boy next to me placed his crutches on the floor and tossed a soft plastic beach-ball-sized ball to a girl in a wheelchair. *I really don't want to be here.*

Just then Coach came over. "How's it going? Give me five."

I smoothed my hand across his palm and he slapped mine back playfully. Then he dribbled a basketball, passing it to me. I watched it roll away. He quickly retrieved it and tried again, throwing it in my lap. "Thanks a lot!" I yelled back, dropping it. "I wasn't ready!"

Coach bounced from foot to foot, his sneakers squeaking across the varnished wood floor. "Come on, Daniel, work on those skills. I want you in regular gym. You hear me?"

"I hear you," I grumbled, starting to get up.

He handed me the ball this time. "Now aim and score."

I leaned on the walker with all my strength. As I aimed for the hoop, my legs tensed from the pressure of not supporting myself on its metal bar with my arms. The basketball didn't even come close to the rim.

"Try again," said Coach, retrieving the ball and handing it to me. Less than a year earlier, he would have casually tossed it at my chest or made me get it myself.

I shot again, missing again. This time he threw the ball back, and it landed in the basket of my walker.

"Three-pointer, Coach."

"Hey, at least *I'm* trying."

"This is dumb." I remembered how Bobby and I used to go at it one-on-one in his driveway as Max chased after the ball, barking.

"What's dumb is not trying."

So I aimed and tossed again.

"Push yourself!" He raised his voice.

"I am!" I shouted back.

On the third try the ball nearly made the net.

"You've still got it!" Coach yelled to me. "You see what you can do if you try?"

I saw Krista running around the folding wall after a stray volleyball. *Did she see me miss the basket?* She scooped up her ball and ran away as quickly she had run in. *Is she going to keep her word about helping me practice swimming? We didn't talk about when to meet. Who's going to call first, her or me?* I had never called a girl before on the phone, not even Krista. *Should I just e-mail? Or work out a time at lunch? Maybe if I bump into her at her dad's office . . .*

Coach had told me to push myself.

I glided the walker across the slick floor. "Coach," I said, "I'm going to—" and I paused. "Push myself." I tapped my fisted knuckles gently against his fist. And Coach, big rough, tough Coach, Coach, Cockroach, cleared his throat. His eyes got a little wet. He swallowed and said nothing. His big, crooked smile said it all.

When I got home, one of the college-age violin students was leaving in a rush, looking distracted and upset. I shouted, "Mom!" There was no answer. "Ma!" I shouted again. "Where are you? You'll be happy to know I saw Coach today!" I searched the rooms. No milk and cookies. No crackers and cheese. Not even a "Hi, sweetie, have a piece of fruit. How was school today?"

Then I stuck my head in her studio. It was dark, except for a stained-glass lamp in the corner that she had picked up in a thrift shop. She was slumped over music scores of her own unfinished compositions spread out on Grandpa's old mahogany desk, the one with the carvings all over the thick wooden legs. Her music stand was set up with some Bach partitas she used to warm up with instead of scales. The cream-colored music book was open to the same one in A major she had been studying before the accident. She hadn't played in a long time, and it made me happy to see the blue velvet interior of her open violin case. I wanted to put my arm around her shoulder, but I remained in the doorway several feet away, which felt like miles. We were like two notes with all those quiet spaces in between.

"Did something happen today, Mom? Just now?" My heart was beating so fast I thought it would explode.

She got up, looking tired, and grabbed my hand, leading me over to the big ottoman, where we both sat down. "You're in school getting back to your own life. That makes me so happy." And she put her hand to her chest and gulped. "Now I have to find my way back. And I'm not sure what that is."

"Oh." I took in a breath. "Look"—I pointed to the partita—"you started playing again. And giving lessons."

She nodded. "I know, honey." She smoothed my hair. "But I've been here every single minute since the . . ." She couldn't even say the word.

"Accident," I completed her sentence. I thought of saying, *Me too,* but I didn't. "So what are you telling me?"

"I feel inside that I just need to get away for a little while. My sister's invited me to come back home and stay at her place in Baton Rouge."

"But this is home. Not Louisiana."

"I know, but I haven't been there in years. Since we

went on a car trip down south when you were much younger. Remember?" She let out a smile, remembering.

I shrugged, the memories vague. "Can't you get away *here*?" I begged. "I'll try not to be a problem."

"Oh, sweetheart." She threw her arms around me and began to sob. "You, a problem?"

"So what was the big speech about hope and getting through things together?" I noticed an airline ticket tucked halfway under some sheets of sonatas. My voice cracked. "And I believed you."

She seemed sad and confused as she fumbled with the tiny electric metronome.

"When are you going?" I tried not to show her my real emotions.

"Tomorrow." She touched my sleeve reassuringly.

"For how long?"

"Just a short break, honey."

"The weekend? A week? What, Ma?"

"I don't have an exact return flight date. I'll let you and Dad know."

"Well, thank Aunt Edna for that book she sent me on famous swimmers while I was recuperating." I got up to leave, pushing onto the walker, denying her efforts to help me. "Oh, and have fun."

"Daniel, please don't be like that." She touched my sleeve.

"Like what?" I said as I left.

• • •

Mom left the next day. We drove her to LaGuardia Airport but didn't go inside. First of all, we weren't allowed at the gate. And even if we were, my mother wanted to go in alone. "If you come with me," she said, "I'm never going to leave. I won't be able to." Her chest heaved when she said that. She bent down and kissed me and stayed several seconds too long in that position, holding me. Then Dad got out, came around the fender, and gave her a big hug and kiss. From inside the car, I waved to her by the curb. She rolled her suitcase with her black violin case strapped over her shoulder and never looked back. She couldn't.

Seven

Krista

Bugs never hang out. They're always going somewhere.
—Jerry Seinfeld, comedian

I rushed past Matt, his pudgy face in the palms of his hands, staring at a glass of orange juice on the kitchen table. He glanced up at me and smiled expectantly. "Not now," I blurted out before he had a chance to say anything. I slammed the door to my bedroom, got out the old candy box buried in my closet, and found the third-grade love note. I unzipped my backpack, took out the scrap of paper Bobby had written on and ripped from his notebook with my name and day for the frog assignment, and compared the scripts. The *K*'s were different, but we'd just been learning cursive in third grade. People's handwriting changes as they get older. I had seen his over the years pinned up in the hall and classroom, but since the famous note, I'd never had a sample in my own hands to inspect up close and personal. Should I consult an expert? I pulled up the online yellow pages and found a listing for a handwriting analyst: *Graphology Detective: We've got the write stuff.*

Friday after school, I got an IM from Sandy. *Want 2 ride bikes?*

What time? I wrote back.

Now. Gina's working at her uncle's. Want ices?

No way! It's November. But I'll tag along.

Stray autumn leaves curled on the sidewalk in front of Sandy's as I waited by the curb. A grass strip separated our houses, which were so close that my mother sometimes picked up our phone to answer it when their phone rang. Once, while I was standing in the tub taking a shower in the one bathroom my family shared, Sandy's older stepbrother, Eric, was getting something from her bedroom exactly opposite our bathroom window, and I think he saw me. Even though I didn't measure a 32A yet, I wanted to die. Eventually Sandy asked, "How come you never come over anymore?" When I got up the nerve to tell her the truth, we did an experiment: I stood in my tub fully clothed, while she peered out her window. "I can only see you from the neck up," she said over the phone. "Now will you come for dinner?" I went, but her brother gave me weird looks during dessert, so I made my mother buy a shade at Bed, Bath & Beyond. To this day, I still can't make full eye contact with Eric.

Sandy's garage door opened and she rode out, her red ponytail bouncing. "Ready?" she asked.

A horn startled me. Lainie stuck her head out her car window. "Where're you two off to?"

"Carmine's," we said together, then mouthed, *Jinx.*

"Elana." Lainie's mother drummed her fingers on the steering wheel, wearing her old wedding band on her middle finger, where it looked too tight. Years ago, they would have been manicured, like Lainie's, but now the nails were bitten and looked uneven and let-go, like the peeling paint on the front shutters of their house.

"Off to a casting call." Lainie batted her long, thick lashes. "For freckle cream. Hey, carrot top, I'll try to pick you up a jar!" she yelled to Sandy, who had pale skin and tons of freckles to go with her hair.

"Did you see her? With a gazillion layers of mascara. My mother would ground me for a month," Sandy shouted over the busy afternoon traffic as we rode to Carmine's.

A line was already forming when we got there. The stand was open year-round and in the winter Carmine served peppermint stick ices and hot chocolate.

My stomach gave a slight tingly turn when we saw Bobby and Brandon waiting for ices, and it probably wasn't the kind of tingle my father described when he hooked Daniel up to those electrodes. Bobby was wearing faded jeans and a jacket from the Gap. Wisps of his sandy-colored hair clung to the back of his collar. I leaned my bike against a fire hydrant. My father had laid down the law that Matt and I would always have to wear helmets. "I've seen too much," he'd insisted when I tried to escape the other day, my shiny auburn hair billowing like in one of those shampoo commercials. Now I felt like a real dork as I tried to look casual and figure out where to hide something that looked appropriate for a liftoff at Cape Canaveral.

Gina waved Sandy and me over to the counter. She was busy scooping a double helping of peanut butter fudge into a cup for Bobby while Brandon was telling one of his jokes. "Two cannibals are eating a clown, and one says to another, 'Does this taste funny?' "

"Everyone knows clowns taste like chicken," Gina said, handing Bobby his change. "My advice, Brandon, is don't take it on the road."

"If I do, want to come?" He wiggled his eyebrows up and down.

Gina plopped a fluorescent green scoop of key lime pie ice in his hand. "On the house," she said with a smirk.

"That's cold." Brandon rushed to get a napkin from the dispenser. "And I don't mean the temperature."

Gina turned to Sandy and me as the boys left, lowering her voice as if she were revealing the secrets of the Dead Sea Scrolls. "I heard rumblings about a party. Meet me in twenty minutes at my house."

We followed Bobby and Brandon into the pizza place next door. They were playing a video game and barely looked at us. My heart sank. I ordered a slice with extra cheese to go.

On the way to Gina's, we passed Daniel's. I placed the grease-stained paper bag on top of his mailbox. Between the screen and front door a large package was propped. The return address label was from Emmaline Rosen, Baton Rouge, Louisiana. I rang the doorbell, then pedaled away as fast as I could. When I turned around, off in the distance, Mr. Rosen was holding the slice of pizza, looking very puzzled.

"He must think the mailman's gone psycho," Sandy said, looking at me as if *I* was the one who was psycho.

"I promised myself I would give Daniel a pizza party when he came home."

"Well, you still owe him, because one measly slice on his stoop doesn't make it."

"You're right." I sighed. "Sandy, I saw something strange by the door."

"Stranger than a slice of pizza?"

"There was a FedEx package from Daniel's mother." As we turned the corner onto Twenty-fifth Avenue, I added, "I wonder why."

"Maybe she's visiting someone?"

"Maybe," I said. "But she seems to live and breathe Daniel. I can't imagine her leaving him even for a few days."

We parked our bikes on a dirt patch near the dying tomato stalks next to Gina's two-family house. Her grandma was outside, picking herbs. She put her hand to my cheek, and her garlic-scented fingers reminded me of the time we ate garlic cloves from her garden. She told us we'd keep vampires away, and we believed it—we were bite-free. But we also kept people away for a whole week.

We waited for Gina in her bedroom. Her uncle had

hand-painted roses on the vanity. Twelve dusty blown-glass animals, which he'd given to her one at a time on each of her birthdays, marched across the mirrored top next to a sports magazine and another on horses.

When Gina came into her room, Sandy pounced on her. "Any news? On the party?"

"Not yet. I'm working on it."

"And," I said, pointing to a tube on her dresser, "since when do you wear makeup?"

Gina, whom I couldn't remember ever seeing in a dress, tried to hide the Earthy Herb concealer.

"Lainie says it brings out the rich tones of my olive skin. And it stays on in water."

"Since when do you listen to Lainie?" I asked. I thought of the practice sessions with Daniel that I'd agreed to. What if Bobby showed up? Maybe I should use makeup too.

"Want to go to the Y after dinner?" Gina suggested. "I'll try it out."

"Tonight? I didn't bring a bathing suit," said Sandy. "I could go home and get one."

Gina casually slid open the bottom drawer of her dresser. "Borrow mine. You'll look like a babe."

Sandy pulled her top down over her stomach. "Oh, I don't know. We're like Laurel and Hardy. I'll look more like Babe in that movie about the pig."

"Oh, come on, Sandy," I said as Gina handed her a plain one-piece. "Babe was cute."

"I have some tank suits." Gina offered her a dark navy one.

Each of us took turns in the bathroom trying on her suits. I picked a purple one. Gina's bra was slung over the top of the shower stall. I was peeking at the label—34B— when a call came from downstairs, "Supper!"

Gina's grandmother made the best lasagna in a one-mile radius. She dished out portions large enough for Queens and half the borough of Brooklyn. "Your mother's at a church fund-raiser tonight, and your father's working overtime. Why everyone's toilet backs up around dinner-time is beyond me."

We giggled, and Gina snorted red sauce out of her nostrils. "Oh my God! A nosebleed!" shouted Nonna, blotting Gina's face with a plaid dishtowel as we laughed harder.

Gina's uncle Carmine came home, gobbled down his meal faster than a termite in a lumberyard, and gave his mother a peck on the cheek. "I'm heading back to the store to do paperwork."

"Could you give us a lift to the Y?" Gina coaxed, looking up pleadingly.

"How could I refuse a face like that?" He squeezed both her cheeks.

At the Y, I undressed in the locker room under a big beach towel, although I didn't have much to hide. Sandy was already wearing the tank suit that she had tried on earlier underneath her clothes. Her extra-large sweat-shirt hung so low, it covered her thighs. I noticed Gina wearing a sports bra. She had shaved her calves and armpits, and saw me staring at her smooth, muscular legs. In contrast, I had light brown wisps sprouting from each follicle like a freshly seeded lawn.

"I'll look prehistoric next to you," I complained to her as we went into the shower.

"Nonna said women in Italy don't shave under their arms," Gina informed us.

A woman with breasts stretched like pulled taffy paraded around the locker room, reminding me of a song the boys used to sing at day camp. *Do your boobs hang low? Do they wobble to and fro? Can you tie them in a knot? Can you tie them in a bow? Can you throw them over your shoulders like a bouncing rubber ball? Do your boobs hang low?* So I figured two things: One, I should buy a bra ASAP. And two, if my breasts ever get like that, I'm going to shoot myself.

I tucked the towel tighter around my body as I opened the frosted glass door to the pool. No boys. It was slightly past dinnertime, so all was still quiet. I jumped in the nearest lane. Gina and Sandy headed toward the other empty ones. I swam back and forth. On my tenth lap, I glanced up and saw Daniel. His father was guiding him in the lane marked SLOW in big black letters. Daniel's legs were flailing while his dad supported him under his stomach. Not the person who won the May Meet last year.

Eight

Daniel

Each night, when I go to sleep, I die.
And the next morning, when I wake up, I am reborn.
—Mahatma Gandhi, spiritual leader of India

When I saw the girls in the other lanes, I said to my father, "Let's go."

"We just got here. You're doing great," he said as I struggled to kick.

Krista saw that I saw her, and waved. Gina and Sandy looked in the direction of that wave, and then followed her as she got out of the pool and came around toward me.

"Hi, Mr. Rosen," they said together, like the Three Musketeers. "Hi, Daniel."

I stayed in the water with the boogie board under my arms, bobbing like a seagull on a buoy. "Hi." I tried to sound casual as my eyes darted to my walker, which was parked near the wheelchair lift that went into the pool.

Gina dipped a toe into my lane. "This must feel good again."

"Well," I muttered, "the way it's going, the class tadpole's gonna beat me."

The girls' expressions tightened and my father looked off to the side.

Krista said thoughtfully, "There's an old children's book my grandfather used to read to me—*The Little Engine That Could*. It's about a little train trying to get over a steep mountain, who says, 'I think I can.'"

But could I? Could I get over that steep mountain? It's weird how things can change after elementary school. Now being friends with a girl was a major plus. I smiled at Krista and she smiled back. She and her friends walked over to the hot tub near the pool and plopped into the water like steamed soup dumplings. I heard their laughter as light bounced off the rippling water in the pool. I floated and drifted, barely moving my arms and legs. Suspended. It felt magical. For the first time in months, I didn't feel trapped inside my body. I looked over at my father watching me. He put his hand to his chest as if he were catching his breath, tapped it twice, and swallowed hard. "It's going to be okay, Dan. You'll see. It's all going to be okay."

"Dad, what's the matter? You're crying."

He wiped the corner of his eye. "No, I'm not."

"Is it Mom? Her not seeing me at the pool?"

"I miss your mother. I miss the three of us, together. Most of all, I missed *you*."

"But I'm here."

"Thank God you're here. I'm getting you back, Daniel." He splashed water at me.

I splashed him, and he rubbed his eyes. "Are you crying again?"

"No! You got chlorine in my eyes," he said, smiling.

"Big blubbering baby," I teased, splashing him again.

We got into a water fight. The lifeguard leaped up and blew the whistle at us. We laughed and continued to fool around until we heard a second whistle. As we got back to the therapy I pretended that my mother was watching on the bleachers, or waiting at home with bowls of coffee ice cream and whipped cream, where we'd replay video of my moves in the pool.

Krista came back to my lane, her cheeks rosy with moisture, and squatted down before she and her friends left. I looked up and said in a low voice, "You want to meet this coming Tuesday?" I was glad Krista didn't ask why I had done my first swim without her—I was lonely because my mother was off on her so-called vacation.

"Tuesday?" she repeated. "Sounds okay."

I was looking forward to swimming again in less than a week. Especially with her. "Krista?"

"Yeah?" She bent over my lane, and I stared into her water-green eyes.

"Don't tell anyone I'm going to work out again. Not a soul."

She looked over at her friends. "But Sandy and Gina know now."

"I mean the heavy-duty practices with you. Who knows, maybe I'll be in the May Meet."

"That's a lot of pressure. On you *and* me."

I looked at her. "Just call me the Little Engine That Could."

"Okay, I won't say anything. I promise. Pinky swear." She kissed her pinky, bringing it away from her lips into the air.

Gina and Sandy came back just then, towels wrapped around them. "We're going to be leaving soon too," my father told them. "Need a lift?"

"That's okay, my uncle's picking us up," said Gina.

On the way home, my father turned on the car radio, which was set to one of Mom's favorite stations. The DJ was playing an old Muddy Waters tune. I pressed the button to change it and got another of her station choices, this one playing bluegrass. *Sweet Jesus got a good thing going.* There was fancy pickin' on the guitar and lyrics about sinners, with the occasional *Oh Lord!* thrown in. I turned to one of the rock stations, and then to talk radio. On the front seat, I pushed aside a postcard of an old Bourbon Street building with a black wrought-iron balcony. It must be from my mother, though I hadn't seen it before.

Dad saw me glance at it. "She e-mailed me last night. She was talking about heading over to Lafayette. Some fiddle player has a music school in his store. They jam Saturday mornings. She sounds more relaxed."

"Cajun Country Day School." I changed the station again.

"Something like that." We stopped at an intersection, and he turned to me. "Daniel, you can count on her."

"I can?"

"She knows this has been horrible for you. Because she loves you so much, it has been really rough on her too. But I think a short break with no responsibilities might do the trick."

"*On her?*" I said as we headed up our street. "How about me? And it's not over yet."

"No, it's not over. After tonight, though, I can see it's a beginning."

He shut off the motor, leaned over, and hugged me.

I looked down at the seat and flipped over the postcard. Couldn't help it.

Dear Bruce,

Hope all is well with you, and that Daniel is busy and thriving.

Has he started his swimming yet? Maybe you'll take him this weekend while I'm gone. I think that will be good for him.

To find who he is again. Like me. It's tough letting go. Let him fly.

We all need to fly in life.

Send him my love. Be brave.

Emma

I was wearing the T-shirt Mom had sent—the one I'd gotten in a package from her earlier today. On the front it said LET THE GOOD TIMES ROLL. On the back was the same thing in French: LAISSEZ LES BON TEMPS ROULER. I was waiting for the good times. "Dad—has she called you yet? Besides sending you this lousy postcard." I was afraid to ask, *When is she coming home?*

He stared straight ahead. "Daniel, it's fine," he said, never saying what the "it" was.

We both sat there in the car saying nothing, but it wasn't a bad quiet. My father rubbed my arm, and then ran his palm across my back and shoulders. It made me think of my mother smoothing the wrinkles out of my gray hooded sweatshirt with the warmth of her hand. A tear dripped down my father's cheek. Then mine. We handed each other tissues, looked into each other's eyes, and smiled. Maybe Mom wasn't the only one who knew how to smooth out the wrinkles.

Nine

Krista

All children, except one, grow up.
They soon know that they will grow up.
—*from* Peter and Wendy, *by James Barrie*

When I got home from the pool, I locked the bathroom door—especially from Matt, who had a habit of barging in on me. How do you remove gorilla fur? Gina's legs had looked sleek, like in one of those ads in *Seventeen* magazine, while mine looked like they should be on the Discovery Channel. I rested my foot on the fluffy beige toilet-seat cover and smeared my father's shaving cream on my legs. My skin stung as I glided his razor upward across the tiny hairs. When I was done, I searched my mother's makeup bag for something to cover the nicks but couldn't find anything. I wanted to try on her mascara, but none was left, so I dipped a dry toothbrush in a jar of Vaseline and brushed a dab on my eyelashes. "Baby, I'm yours," I sang to my reflection in the mirror, batting my lashes as if I were Lainie, tweenage model.

A few minutes later, while I was getting ready for bed,

I heard Matt let out a scream. "What's this gunk on my new red toothbrush? *Mommy!*"

I hopped under the blanket, looking as innocent as I could when my mother came into my room and lowered the shades. Band-Aids dotted my calves and ankles beneath my plaid flannel drawstring pants, hiding the dried blood of my accidental cuts.

"Can you leave them up? It's a full moon tonight," I asked.

"A harvest moon—like a slice of orange. Hmmm, someone's a romantic."

"Mom!" I whined, making a face.

She lifted the shades. Leafy patterns danced along the walls through lace curtains. She tucked the quilt around me, then sat on the bed, and I rolled to face her. She smelled of jasmine and leftover meat loaf. I closed my eyes, absorbing her scent. It made me think of Daniel's mother and how she often smelled like her herb garden from weeding, pruning, planting, and how this year it had become overgrown with weeds. The rust, orange, and burgundy mums that lined the Rosens' front stoop each fall were absent. A wind chime remained dangling on its broken nylon string. I would miss my mother's smell if she went away.

"Mom, did Mrs. Rosen go on a vacation? Or leave home?"

"She ran away with a little knapsack slung over her shoulder."

"I mean it, Ma."

"I know you do." She took in a breath. "Maybe Emma needed time off from being a caretaker. I think she's an artistic, sensitive soul who has always felt oppressed by her suburban mom lifestyle. You know she's a classically trained violinist from Juilliard. We don't really know what she's going through, do we? Life is complicated. Things happen."

I thought of when I'd sometimes ride by Daniel's house and hear sweet sounds coming out of it, Beethoven, or Mozart, or Chopin. And when I used to visit on a play date and we'd dance in the living room to wilder music. She never said "Stop." She turned up the volume.

Mom paused. "She called me from the airport before she left, asking me to help out in case Daniel or his dad needed anything. His father has to work."

"So do you," I said. "So you're the backup, like in the cop shows."

"No one could be a backup for Emma. She's one of a kind. And I'm not worried about Bruce. He's a great father."

"Ma . . ." I hesitated. "Did you ever want to leave us?"

"Oh, sweetie, at least once a day."

"Gee, thanks a lot."

"Don't worry. I'm not going anywhere." My mother stroked my back through the blanket. "You know this Navajo throw we got during our trip to New Mexico?" I nodded, glancing at the foot of my bed. "There's one thin line out of whack with the rest of the pattern."

"A mistake?"

"No. The weaver deliberately adds it into the design. It's known as the spirit path. Without that line that strays to the edge, the artist's spirit can become trapped in the blanket. And therein lies the imperfect dilemma of motherhood. Someday, when you're a mother, a wife, and something special in the world, you'll understand."

My mother's face looked beautiful in the moonlight. I imagined her young.

"Ma, did you ever have a crush on someone?"

"Your father."

I rolled my eyes.

"Mom, I mean *someone*."

"That's right, I forgot—Dad's not a person. What could I have been thinking?"

"Mom," I said again. "You know what I mean."

She gave a wide grin. "David Lloyd Fisher."

"You still remember his *middle* name?"

"Not only that, I remember he sat in the middle of the fifth row in front of me. He was shorter than me by about an inch, but then most boys are shorter than girls in fourth grade."

"Fourth grade!" I screamed.

She put her hand over my mouth as if we were at a pajama party, which in a way we were. "What can I tell you? I was advanced for my age."

I thought of liking Bobby since third grade, so I guess that put me ahead of her.

"He had big blue eyes and light brownish hair like your father. I used to stare at the back of his head for hours as I sat behind him. During arithmetic. During spelling. During lunch. You name it. When he gave me an engagement ring out of the bubble gum machine from the corner candy store, I was putty in his hands for the entire year. Although I would have been crazy about him if he had given me nothing. I still have that ring in my jewelry box."

"You do?" I was shocked.

"One husband and two kids later, I do. And it's the only diamond I own."

I smiled, thinking of the note I had kept in my valentine box. Then I touched Mom's engagement ring with the delicate, smoky green stone in the center.

"Dad gave it to me while I was eating a greasy lamb chop. It was from an antique store—it was all he could afford." She slipped it off her finger and held it up to the moonlight. "The words 'To Mother from Ronald' were engraved on the inside of the band. Most of the words disappeared when it was sized for my ring finger. Just the 'Mother' remains. I guess that's fitting now." She put it on my finger. "I don't need diamonds. I have you, your brother, and your father. So I guess I have my diamonds already."

"Oh," we both said together, sticking our fingers down our throats, pretending to gag.

"Do you know what happened to David? Do you ever think about him now?"

"Krista, honey, who has time to think? Between working and raising a family, I would like to have time to think about your father." Then she looked into my eyes. "By the time we were in junior high, David, who now liked to be called Dave, fell madly in love with Frances Kellerman. Fran got a sheepdog that she walked by his house about every hour on the hour. You'd think that dog had a urinary tract problem. Fran wore a training bra prematurely and was the most popular girl in the grade for the entire year."

"What was she training for?"

"Not dog walking, that's for sure. By the end of seventh grade, neglected, I started to pine for Marc Albertson, who had the hots for Cynthia Blair because she wore slinky mohair sweaters and miniskirts the size of a large dinner napkin."

"Like Lainie."

"Exactly. There will always be Lainies. And the boys who have crushes on them. You can count on that. As one gets older, turquoise mohair isn't enough to build a long-lasting relationship. Kindness, respect, trust, someone who's there for you when you need them—that's love. Unconditional love." She moved closer to me. "It'll happen. You'll see. Someday."

I put my arms around my mother's neck and hugged her, tight.

Dad walked in and kissed us both on top of our heads. I felt myself sink deeper into the mattress as if I were being rocked to sleep in a hammock, anchored between two sturdy oaks. I knew that no matter where I was or what I did, my parents would always love me. Someday, maybe someone else would too. That person was out there, somewhere, breathing and living. Like me.

Ten

Daniel

The only joy in the world is to begin.
—Cesare Pavese, poet and novelist

"Your father let you come alone?" was the first thing out of Krista's mouth when she saw me waiting in the lobby at the Y on Tuesday.

"I told him to drop me off at the entrance, that the lifeguard who was on duty the last time we were here was going to help me swim. Just as I was scanning my membership card, the lifeguard walked in and waved."

"What luck." Krista put away a laminated pass with her photo on it. She tilted her head to one side. "Meet you at the pool. You'll be okay?"

I looked at her the way parents look at their kids when they say something really dumb. "Are you offering to come with me in the men's locker room?"

"Just asking. So kill me." She gave me a little wave over her shoulder, her back to me, as we separated to change. I tried to grab the handle of the locker room door and fumbled. *What am I getting myself into? But it feels right. Right for me. Is it right for her?*

Luckily, Krista wasn't in the pool when I used the lift to lower myself into the first lane. The lifeguard rose from a lawn chair and was heading in my direction when Krista appeared in the next lane. She dipped under the long rope that separated the lanes and swam up beside me. "It's cool. I'm with him," she yelled out.

The lifeguard went back to her chair, not taking her eyes off us. Krista pushed her bathing cap up over her ears, dunked under the water, then flipped on her back like an otter and splashed me.

"So you want to play rough?" I flicked water at her with one hand while I held on to the side of the pool with the other. The tiles edging the pool were cool beneath my fingers.

"Hey!" Krista dove under the water, then resurfaced, making swirls with her hand, creating a whirlpool. She had a devilish grin as her hand rotated in faster and faster circles.

"Okay, I see where this is heading," I said with a smile. "Lay off."

She put her hand to her ear. "Can't hear you. It's s-o-o crowded here tonight."

We splattered each other as if we were five years old and in the wading pool, the years suddenly erased. Except now, a tiny pearl dangled from a gold chain around her neck.

"You win, Daniel. Truce!"

"Gee, I can't hear you. It's s-o-o crowded here tonight," I mimicked her.

"Are you ready, barracuda?" she asked.

"Who you calling a barracuda?" I took off without her.

Krista easily caught up to me as I held on to the kickboard, arms extended, legs trying to propel me. She stood and walked beside me, hands ready to catch me while I swam. Once, afraid that I'd go down, she nearly grabbed the waistband of my bathing suit. After a while, we rested, and I slicked back a few stray hairs that had fallen into my eyes.

"Your hair's getting long again. You'll have to wear a bathing cap soon." She touched the side of my head.

"Hey." I jerked away. "Thought we were in a truce mode."

"We are. We definitely are," Krista assured me.

When we started to swim again, she followed behind me. We did almost a lap before I stopped abruptly. Krista bumped into me as I panted, out of breath.

"Take five." She floated next to me in the lane.

A woman tried to pass us. "Are you two socializing or swimming? This is for people who want to do laps, you know."

"I know," I muttered, wanting to shout at the top of my lungs, *A year ago you would have been eating my dust! I wouldn't have been in this lame lane, you old fart.*

A beginner class was leaving the kiddie pool. They wore water wings and puffy floats sewn into their bathing suits. "Remember being them?" I asked.

She nodded.

"Should we try again before the old fart returns?"

Krista nodded once more.

But I was tired. My legs weakened, and I began to sink. Krista held me gently under my arm. Just then I saw Bobby standing on the deck at the end of our lane, his piercing stare directed at Krista and me. I didn't know how long he had been there, watching us. *What's he doing here at night? Bobby usually practices right after school.*

Krista let go and I dipped slightly below the surface again, getting water up my nose. I wanted to beam myself to another planet like they do on *Star Trek*. Then Bobby dove into the pool, heading directly toward us. I froze. So did Krista.

"You okay?" he asked.

I nodded, my nose stinging from the chlorine.

"Because you didn't look too good out there."

"Thanks a lot," I said.

"Can I share the lane?" he asked us.

"Sure. It's a free country."

As Bobby swam ahead of us, Krista continued next to me, which felt annoying now, because I didn't want Bobby to even think for a minute how bad I was, and that Krista—or anyone—might be helping me. He eased up and fell in line on the other side of me. None of us said a word as we swam, Bobby on one side, Krista on the other, with me making headway between them. We moved in one straight line like the three stars of Orion's belt.

As Krista and I were leaving the pool, Coach came in

with some of the team. He waved when he saw me. I acted as if Krista and I weren't together while he began to set up for a local meet, stringing flags across the pool. Before I went into the locker room, I turned around to see Bobby dive into one of the fast lanes, breaking the surface of the still water. That's when I overheard two new boys on the team talking.

"Isn't that the kid who used to be on the team?" one whispered to the other, but I heard him loud and clear. "You know, the one who got crippled from Bobby's father."

Crippled? I went into the locker room and called my father on my cell phone. I couldn't get out of there fast enough.

"Fifteen minutes, okay?" Dad sounded harassed. "Need any help?"

"No." My voice cracked, almost giving me away. "I'm good," I lied.

"All right, then. I'll meet you at the entrance."

While I was getting dressed, Bobby hurried in, stopping dead in his tracks. "Hey."

"Hey." I tried to avoid his glance but couldn't.

He quickly opened his locker and searched through it.

"What?" I said, without thinking, acting as if we were still good friends.

"Can't find my towel. Must have left it home." He shivered.

"Who are you racing tonight?" I asked as I put on my tube socks.

"Burr Intermediate. That new school. You know." He stopped himself.

"I know. The one built over the summer near the high school. I heard about it. I'm not totally out of it. Are they any good?"

"Not like us." He looked up at me, then looked down again.

Us.

"Want to borrow my towel? Better than nothing." I could see he was considering it. I pushed it toward him on the long wooden bench in front of the lockers. "Take it, Bobby."

"Okay. Thanks. I'll return it."

"Don't worry about it. It's my old Snoopy beach towel."

He opened it up and laughed. "I'm going to look like a doofus."

"Hey," I said, "you can handle it."

He glanced at my walker, which was leaning against the locker, as he wrapped the towel around his waist. I slammed the locker door and zipped up my duffel bag, ready to leave.

"Daniel?" he said, and I glanced over. "I'm having a party after Thanksgiving. For the holidays. I hope you come." He paused. "My parents will be around. Just wanted you to know that." That was Bobby's way of saying his father would be there. "You don't have to let me know now. I haven't sent out the e-mails yet."

"Thanks," I said. *For giving me a heads-up.*

Minutes later, while I was waiting in the lobby, I saw Krista. "Guess the cat's out of the bag."

"Don't worry, Daniel." But she looked worried.

We headed outside, and I asked my father, "Can you give Krista a lift? We bumped into each other at the pool." I hoped my mother hadn't told him Krista might help me. That way, if I failed at what I was trying to do, then no one would know, except Krista and me—and now Bobby.

"Sure." He seemed distracted, the way parents get when they're not really listening to what you're saying, which sometimes feels like most of the time.

Dad didn't talk like his usual friendly self, so I was relieved to see the familiar pine-green shutters of Krista's small ranch house framing her cat, Rosie, who was sitting in the window.

"Thanks for dropping me off, Mr. Rosen." She leaped out of the car and leaned toward my window. I lowered it. "See you in school, Daniel." She stepped over a pile of scarlet and gold leaves under the large maple tree her father tapped each February. He invited the neighborhood kids over and served pancakes with his homemade syrup, which he boiled in the backyard on his grill. I once ate a dozen.

My father waited with me by the curb in the car until she got safely inside.

Krista rang the doorbell, and a moment later her mother flipped on the light over the front door and let her in. She kissed Krista's cheek and patted her on the back. I brushed my eyes with the back of my hand so Dad wouldn't see the tear. I knew it was dumb to compare my life to someone else's. That sort of thing doesn't ever get you anywhere—anywhere but feeling bad, or feeling better because that person is in bad shape. Really, what good does it do? But just then I wanted to be standing in my foyer, the light shining on me, and my mom planting a kiss on my cheek. "Be careful what you wish for," Mom would often say. I thought of all the times I'd wanted her to disappear to Mars or at least to Staten Island, with a river or two between us. That was then. There's always a then. And a now.

Eleven

Krista

The whole of life lies in the verb seeing.
—*Pierre Teilhard de Chardin, Jesuit priest,*
philosopher, and paleontologist

My mind went round and round like a whirling dervish about Bobby, Daniel, and me. Bobby in his Hawaiian bathing suit. His blue eyes the color of water. His skin glistening. How I'd tossed my hair when I lifted myself up the ladder out of the pool, like I had seen Lainie do at least a hundred times. And how he'd waved good-bye to me and smiled one of those movie star smiles. I nearly fell out of my bed when the door slammed and my dad screamed, "Hey, I'm back with some pizza!"

"I pass," I called out from my room. Now that I was swimming again, I had to consider Number 6 on my list: lose five pounds or else maybe I was never going to see Number 7 happen—"The Kiss."

A while later, Matt came in holding a slice, sauce plastered all over his face and hands. "I saved a piece for you." Cheese oozed onto the plush carpet.

"Don't touch a thing!" I cried out, taking him directly to the bathroom, away from my bedspread. His dinosaur slipper roared when I stepped on a big yellow toe, the size of a banana, and I reached for a new bar of soap in the cabinet under the sink.

My mother stood in the hallway watching me scrub him. "I'm happy you're my children and no one else's."

"You'll want to get rid of one of us when you see my carpet."

She put down the basket of folded laundry and pulled us both toward her in a sandwich hug. "Carpets can be cleaned."

Later that night, I went online to the unofficial Krista-Sandy-Gina-Lainie chat room. This is the super-short version:

> **Headshot** (Lainie): Got the commercial!!! Shooting on South Beach over Thanksgiving at the Delano. It's the cool one where all the celebrities go. Lobby and pool—like a movie set.
>
> **TuttiFrutti** (Gina): There'll be no talking to you, Lain. Better stay grounded. We're going to the Jersey Shore. Uncle Carmine wants to see if he should open another ices place this summer.
>
> **Freckleface** (Sandy): Doing college tours. Looking around, Eric the

Ferret's applying to—get this—fifteen! None early admission. I read one of his personal essays on the difficulties of not being in a nuclear family, even though I wasn't supposed to, but he hid it under his thesaurus—and I happened to need another word for "ubiquitous."

Headshot: Welcome to America.

TuttiFrutti: Give me a break. Nuclear smuclear. At least he didn't write on helping underprivileged children in some Latin American country when he was really on spring break in Costa Rica.

Freckleface: His grammar and vocabulary were good. Nice sentence structure.

Headshot: Hate grammar. Check out the journal on the freckle cream blog, Lentigo.com.

TuttiFrutti: Huh? Like in those brown lentils Nonna cooks in her soups?

Freckleface: It's a synonym for freckle. Just looked it up in Eric's thesaurus.

Biobuff (Krista): See, he's good for
something.

I kept quiet about the swim, like Daniel asked me to,
and about Bobby. How come I wasn't sharing with my
best friends? What was happening to me? Was this what
growing up was like—breaking away and being close at
the same time? I shut down my computer and prepared
my outfit for the next morning.

Wednesday was Lainie's day with the tadpole. "Come and
get it!" she exclaimed in homeroom before science class,
giving the tadpole a pinch of dried worms. She marked
down on the chart: *Hind legs developing.*

"Yummy," Gina said, passing Lainie. "By the way, did
you e-mail the entire planet about the commercial? Because in the last twelve hours everyone in the world
seems to know." She rolled her eyes as I shook my head.
"And eight of those hours we were all sleeping."

Lainie gave Gina a look.

"You know I'm right," Gina insisted, looking over at me.

I knew she was.

"Krista, are you coming?" Gina asked as Lainie acted
real busy, putting away frog food on a shelf under the
tank. As she got up, she tripped over a backpack on the
floor.

"Sorry, it was mine," Bobby admitted. She leaned on
him as he helped her to her feet.

My eyes rested on them. His arm on hers. Hers on his. *Them.*

"I twisted my ankle," Lainie moaned. "The commercial!"

Gina gave me a you-see-what-I-mean look. Lainie took off her sneaker and polka-dot sock and propped her leg up on a chair. Gina stared at the silver toe ring on Lainie's middle toe. "No wonder you fell."

"Give me a break." Lainie massaged her foot. "Like *that* would make me fall."

"Anyway, what's the big deal? Are they filming freckles on your ankle?" Gina asked.

"No, but who wants a gimp on the set?" Lainie glared at Gina, and then we all looked in Daniel's direction as he came into the classroom. It got very quiet. I prayed he hadn't heard her snide remark, but judging by his face, I think he had.

More and more people came into homeroom, and Lainie was enjoying the attention. We had a substitute teacher that day, who asked, "Do you need to go to the nurse?"

Lainie played it up. "I'll be okay," she sighed, adding, "hopefully."

"Are you okay?" Bobby asked.

Gina mumbled under her breath, "I think she'll live."

"Thanks, Bobby," Lainie replied, rubbing her ankle even more. "At least *someone* cares." She glared over at Gina.

But I was stuck on the way Bobby helped her. I think *he* cared.

A bell rang. "Great, a fire drill," Lainie said. "Go

ahead, I'll catch up with you." She made an effort to get up and limped slowly toward the door.

"She's milking this for all it's worth," Gina insisted as we headed downstairs single file. "She should switch from modeling to acting. She'd win an Academy Award."

"Oh, Gina," Sandy sighed.

"Don't 'Oh, Gina' me. She's always falling. Anything for attention. I *hate* that."

"Maybe she really did trip," I said.

"Fire drill!" shouted Brandon happily. "No math quiz next period!"

"Did you pull the lever?" asked Gina. "To get out of the exam. It's a crime, you know."

"Shh! Quiet and orderly," the substitute teacher instructed in her teacher tone.

All grades hurried to the exits, lining up against the chain-link fence in the schoolyard. As we waited for everyone to come out, I turned toward Gina and Sandy. "Where's Daniel?"

"And Lainie?" asked Sandy, looking around.

I ran to the front of the line to tell the substitute. She paled. "Watch my class!" she shouted to another teacher, then rushed to a side door. Classes continued to empty from the building. *What if this is for real?* I thought, suddenly afraid.

Minutes felt like hours, waiting. Then I saw Lainie and Daniel trudging out the door. A small plastic tank with a bobbing palm tree was in the front basket of Daniel's walker. They were both hobbling, using his walker together. I ran toward them. "Are you okay?"

"With me limping, and Daniel, well, you know, and the sub off to who knows where, no one seemed to remember *us*," Lainie said in a huff, reaching for a tissue. She blew her nose in a dramatic gesture as Daniel stared down at the blacktop.

Coach rushed over with the substitute by his side. She was shaken up. Almost in tears, she kept repeating, "I checked for everyone."

"Obviously not," Coach told her brusquely.

"But the room seemed empty," she protested.

"What if this wasn't a drill?" he went on. "Daniel and Lainie could have died."

"This is my first day, my first hour here," she said sheepishly.

"You okay, big guy?" Coach put his arm around Daniel.

Daniel shrugged. "I'm fine."

Lainie joined in. "I was in the coat closet getting my jacket on, hopping on one foot, while Daniel was saving the tadpole in case this wasn't just a dumb drill."

Coach cut Lainie off as he looked at Daniel. "In a real fire, the elevator would have been brought down to the first floor and service would be discontinued. You're supposed to head to a safe stairwell and wait until a rescue team comes. Don't take this the wrong way, but for now, don't be such a hero."

The rest of the day, Daniel was just that—a hero. A hero is someone who acts without thinking in a crisis to do good. And all were safe. Him. Lainie. The tadpole.

At lunch, Lainie repeated the story to anyone who

84

would listen while the school nurse supplied fresh bags of ice from the cafeteria for her swollen ankle. The story got bigger and bigger with each telling, as if it were the Great Chicago Fire. Outdoors at noontime, she and Daniel were circled by a crowd. Later, while we waited for our buses, people treated her like a star.

"Look at her," Gina said as Lainie flashed her white choppers, flipping her thick blond hair every which way. "She's more popular than ever." The worst part was that Bobby helped her onto the school bus, carrying her backpack. Why did I remain friends with Lainie?

That night at the dinner table, I went on and on about the fire drill, Lainie, and Daniel.

Matt, whose elementary school was next to ours, perked up. "Were there fire engines? And pumps? And big hoses?"

"None. False alarm." I impatiently pushed his snotty damp tissue aside.

"Goody." He sighed with relief. "I didn't miss anything."

After dinner, I helped my dad clean up, stacking the dishes in the dishwasher. As he rinsed a plate he said, "Tell Lainie to come and see me if her ankle acts up."

"Okay. She's worried that she won't be able to do this commercial she got."

"Her mother will freak out if she can't," said Mom. "I think I'm going to start a new organization—Parents Without Borders—and make Mildred my first member."

My father looked at my mother and snickered as he scrubbed a pot.

While my mother was heating the teakettle, Dad put

85

out plates for dessert. Matt dragged out his blanket and stuffed bear and tried to sit on my lap. He rubbed his eyes. I ignored him, trying to push him off. "What are you doing, Pest Breath?"

"Ma!" Matt yelled. "Krista's making fun of me."

"And he's bothering me. His blanket smells like old sour milk."

Matt began to whimper, and he tried to kick me, but I was too big for him to win.

Mom glanced at Dad and then at us. "Now you know why some animals eat their young."

When I went into Matt's room after Mom and Dad tucked him in for the eightieth time, his eyes widened. "Could you read me a story, Krista?"

"If it is *Bugs Bunny's Birthday,* forget it. A *good* story."

"Okay, Krista. Then tell me a good story."

"Once upon a time, there was a rabbit who had everything in the entire world—a berry bush, a thick patch of straw to sleep on, and all the alfalfa it could ever want in the hay barn."

"Oh, goody, it's still a bunny."

"And," I continued as his lids began to droop, "it wanted more."

"But you said the rabbit had everything."

"Just listen." I snuggled closer. "Everyone always wants more."

"Too bad," Matt said, drifting off. "All Bugs Bunny ever wants is a big juicy carrot."

I wanted to be seven again. Or Bugs Bunny.

Twelve

Daniel

*People wish to learn to swim and at the same time
to keep one foot on the ground.*
—Marcel Proust, author

The following day, Lainie sat out recess with me. My popularity went off the charts. Although if she was with a tarantula, everyone would probably want one as a pet.

"I'm shooting a commercial over Thanksgiving."

"I know." Everyone knew.

"Are you visiting your mother? Where is she again?" Lainie blurted out.

"I'm staying home with my father. And the tadpole. Mr. James is letting me frog-sit."

"Guess he heard how we rescued the tadpole."

I grimaced, thinking, *I took it during the fire drill, not her.*

Bobby tossed Brandon a basketball, and Brandon cried out as Gina walked past the court, "Hey, Deluca, want a little horizontal one-on-one?"

If looks could kill, Brandon was second in line after Lainie on Gina's hit list. Or possibly first.

My father came at the end of the day to get the stuff for the tadpole. It was a few days before break, but it was the only time he could squeeze in to come by. His shirt and tie looked rumpled, and he seemed tired from being in court all day, but he still forced a smile when he came into our classroom. Mr. James mouthed to him, *He's doing great.*

We went straight from school to my physical therapy appointment with Krista's father. Dad handed me a vanilla milkshake. "I'll get you in an hour. I have forensic work to do on a case," he said as Mr. Harris let me in.

"Don't forget to put the tadpole in the house."

I made my way to the ballet bar. Mr. Harris fastened light weights to my ankles. I counted, "One, two, three, four," as I held on to the long wooden bar, slowly doing leg lifts in front of a mirror hung low along the wall. Krista came downstairs. She fell into the beat of the CD, doing leg lifts alongside me. As we got into a quicker tempo, her smile broadened. So did mine. I could feel myself getting stronger. "My aim," I said, leaning over the bar, "is *never* to come here again."

"You don't like us?" she teased. "I promise I won't make you wear a tutu."

"Like I'm *ever* going to wear a short skirt. Truthfully, I prefer swimming to ballet."

Krista looked into my eyes. "I understand."

I tried lifting my leg a little higher in rhythm with the music.

"What are you doing over Thanksgiving?" she asked. "Anything special?"

"Frog-sitting. Watching the parade on TV. Eating turkey. Probably a DVD."

"Me too. Nothing special. Everyone's leaving."

"Not me." I waited for her to say, *Maybe we could hang out together?* But she didn't.

And neither did I.

When I got home and followed my father into the kitchen, the tadpole's tank was by the answering machine. The red light was blinking. I pressed the button to hear the messages. "Hi. It's me, Mom. Wanted to know how you're doing. I'll call back. Love you."

The words "love you" stayed in my head.

The phone rang. Dad yelled from the den, "Could you get that? I'm busy."

I waited for the answering machine to pick up, thinking it was Mom again. I didn't know if I wanted to talk to her.

"Hello?" said my mother's voice. "Is anyone there?"

"I think it's for you!" I shouted to my father.

A few minutes later, Dad called, "Daniel—it's your mother."

I hesitated as I picked up the receiver.

"Hello?" It was my mother's voice again, sounding chipper, like a little bird.

"Hello," I answered. Somehow I couldn't say the word *Mom,* like in "Hello, Mom."

"It's good to hear your voice. How are you, darling? You can't imagine how much I miss you."

"Well, I'm still here."

"Dad told me you're doing great. That you're swimming again."

Dead silence.

"I'm playing with a band at the Turkey Trot Square Dance."

"That's nice," I lied.

"I had hoped the two of you would come here."

"Dad's been on overload with a big case." I tried to make her feel guilty. "So he can't get away."

"I know." She breathed into the phone. "Maybe another time. We can eat crawfish and jambalaya. I want to take you on a swamp boat ride to see alligators in the bayou and to an island where the floats are stored in a warehouse during the year for Mardi Gras."

Like that's going to happen.

"So I guess you're not coming back for Thanksgiving?" My voice rose.

"I'm sorry, sweetheart, but I need some more time," my mother said apologetically.

"Then take it." And I hung up.

The phone rang immediately. I ignored it. Dad answered it but didn't call out to me again. I looked into the tadpole's tank. It swam around the little plastic palm tree, poking its head in between the tiny pebbles. *In my next life, I'm coming back as a frog. It's simpler. And my biggest*

worry will be, do I circle left or right, or go up or down? And
where are my dried worms and flies?

My father came into the kitchen, looked at me, and then glanced away.

"Aren't you mad she's not coming home for Thanksgiving?" I asked.

He took out a frying pan and put it on the stove. He certainly seemed upset.

"What's going on with Mom? When is she coming back?"

"She says she needs space."

"Then let's buy her a one-way ticket to Jupiter. And I don't mean Jupiter, Florida."

"Daniel." Dad glanced over the rim of his eyeglasses, which he wore only for reading.

"So this isn't some little visit to Aunt Edna's anymore, is it?"

Dad sighed. "No."

"Then what is it?" My voice sounded bitter.

His shoulders slumped as he began peeling an onion. "I'm not sure yet."

We had gotten into the habit of making dinner together when he came home from work, but that evening I left him to do it alone. I didn't care about his special deep-fried, battered chicken smothered in gravy with whipped sweet potatoes. I went into my room and slammed my walker into the wall, denting the Sheetrock. It fell on its side next to my desk, and I left it there. I went online, opening my e-mail even though most of it was junk these past months. I found a message from my mother:

From: <u>violinmom</u>
To: <u>danielrosen</u>

I'm sorry, sweetheart, that I've hurt you, because that is not my intention.
    Far from it. Someday I hope that you will understand.
                Love always, Mom XXX

There was another one, this time from Bobby:

Winter Chill

Holiday party at Bobby Kaufman's house
Friday, December 21 at 7:30 p.m.
RSVP

For the first time, I was glad my mother was gone, because she would have had a fit when she heard how I replied to the RSVP: yes.

Thirteen

Krista

In the factory we make cosmetics, in the store we sell hope.
—Charles Revson, president and chairman of Revlon

The big news was the invitation to Bobby's party. It was all
we talked about in our chat room that night.

"Did you get the invitation?" I asked.

Gina shot over, "Told you so. Just didn't know *who* was
having the party."

And with that, Lainie zinged back, "Let's go into the
city to buy ensembles. Not just any old thing at the mall—
one-of-a-kind vintage outfits on Avenue A and B near
St. Marks Place. Don't tell a soul. We'll say to our parents
we're going into Flushing to eat dim sum and that we're
poking around for fabric and bangle bracelets instead of
telling them our real destination: downtown Manhattan."

Saturday morning we took the bus to Main Street to catch
the number seven train. When we got our MetroCards,

I noticed a driver's license in Lainie's plum leather wallet.

"Is that your mother's?" I was confused. "It has your name on it."

Gina grabbed the license to take a closer look. "I don't believe it." She handed it back to Lainie.

"What?" Sandy asked as the train came. "What don't you believe?"

"It's a fake ID," said Gina, staring at Lainie. "You made it over the Internet, I bet."

Sandy's mouth gaped open.

Lainie put the license safely back in her wallet. "Lighten up. I didn't kill anyone. It'll help me get into places when I'm away in Miami, and also with what I want to do today."

"And what's that?" Gina smirked. "You don't have to be over eighteen to get a black strapless dress."

"A tattoo."

"A what?" The three of us screamed so loud everyone on the subway car stared.

"You heard me. I'm getting a tattoo in the East Village," declared Lainie.

"Maybe you didn't kill anyone, but your mother's gonna kill you," insisted Gina.

My mother's aunt Masha had a tattooed number on her arm from when she was in a concentration camp during World War II. She had said with horror when her own daughter wanted to get a tattoo, "Jews don't defile themselves." But Lainie wasn't Jewish. So she wouldn't understand a tattoo was a very sensitive issue in my house—something you just would never do.

"What about the commercial?" I asked tentatively, trying to talk her out of it. "Couldn't having the tattoo hurt you?"

"What does that have to do with anything?" she said impatiently.

"It might have to do with *where* you're having it done," Gina added.

"I'm hiding it on my ankle or shoulder. Maybe the back of my neck."

"You'd better decide carefully, so your mother won't see it," offered Sandy.

"Please," Lainie begged as we changed trains, "back me up on this. It will be a teeny-tiny one. You'll all be incredibly jealous."

"I don't think so." Gina snickered. "I don't like to use my skin as a canvas."

Once we were in Manhattan, in the East Village, we passed cafés with groups of people in their twenties hanging out sipping lattes, boutiques selling everything from colorful saris and silk-embroidered pillows to high-end designer stuff no one could afford. On one street was a seemingly endless row of Indian restaurants, each with a man outside eager to get us to go in and try a big lunch buffet with soup and dessert for only $4.95. Nearby were spice shops, delis the size of postage stamps, and street vendors selling everything from teak incense holders and Tibetan bells to old records, CDs, and comics.

Lainie dragged us into the first tattoo parlor she saw. A craggy-faced man—"or possible pirate," Gina whispered, sparking our giggles—was at the counter. He smiled at Lainie. Anyone would smile at Lainie. She could hold the attention of a flea.

Another man, probably the owner, parted a glass-beaded curtain and saw us. "Come back in a few years."

"But—" Lainie protested, about to pull out her fake ID.

He cut her off, indicating a notice visible in bold type-face over the back door: MUST BE OVER EIGHTEEN. "Jail-bait. I'm not having the Health Department come down on me."

Lainie decided not to argue and continued down the street where a sign was posted: BODY ARTIST. CUSTOM DESIGNS. The three of us followed her inside. Lainie browsed through a black leather portfolio. She pointed to a tribal sun like the one woven in the Native American blanket that hung in my front hall at home. "How much is this?"

"Three hundred bucks. Five hundred if you want it bigger—takes more time."

Lainie blanched. "Thank you."

We quickly left his studio and headed into a hole-in-the-wall storefront two doors down. A guy with his sleeves rolled up, revealing a patchwork of intertwining snakes and dragons on his forearm, was totally taken in when Lainie flashed her pearly whites and then for a brief second her license, which he barely looked at. All he had to do was check out the rest of us without makeup, but I don't think he noticed us. He only saw Lainie—twelve going on twenty, who got away with more than anyone I knew. Without her mascara, eyeliner, and blush, anyone with some left-brain activity would have known the truth. Or been arrested.

"What do you think?" Lainie pointed to a fairy, a ladybug, and a butterfly. "They *are* very small." She looked at Sandy, Gina, and me for approval. "They are."

"You can make it as big or as little as you want," the man said. "If you want a stock, flash piece like that one," he said, showing her a tiny heart, "it will take fifteen minutes for about fifty bucks. Cash up front."

Lainie peeked in her purse and recounted her money. "That's nearly all I have."

"It sounds *very* cheap," I said, "for a tattoo. Not that I would know."

"Is this place okay?" Sandy whispered, as though we'd stepped into some den of iniquity.

"If you want to get an instant case of tetanus it is." Gina tapped her booted foot.

"Are you sure about this, Lain?" I asked. "Seems like a sketchy tattoo parlor to me."

"Because once you do this, you can't change your mind afterward," Gina said, putting in her two cents. "This isn't ordering flavors. You know how many times I've dumped a cup of vanilla for chocolate because a customer can't make up their mind. But hey, that's ices, not some guy's initials in a heart forever. Like BK and LM."

What does Gina mean by that? My heart sank.

Lainie ignored her, looking over at Sandy and me. "A flower or a star?"

"It's your decision." I prayed it wasn't a heart with Bobby's initials inside.

Sandy sighed. "Too many choices. Maybe wait?"

Lainie plunked down the amount—her savings from a magazine print ad. "The star."

"Number thirty-two it is," the man said. He shrank the star in the copy machine and redrew it on tracing paper. Then he put it through another machine, which turned the image purple. Lainie nodded. He brought her to a tattoo station in the rear of the store, where she took a seat in a big red barber's chair. Sandy and I stood by her side. Lainie was too shy to have it done on her hip or breast by a complete stranger, although that would have been totally out of view, for now.

"The back of my neck under my hair, hidden from my mother," ordered Lainie.

"Are you one hundred percent sure?" Gina tossed off. "What about when the weather gets warm? You like to put your hair up in a ponytail or back with a barrette."

Lainie cocked her head. "The ankle, then?"

"Sandals," said Gina from her spot in the corner. "Remember those hot-pink flip-flops you wear to death."

"Right. I forgot. Then the back of my shoulder. Right. No, left." Lainie looked at Gina, whose face remained blank. "No, right shoulder." The man sprayed the area with green soap, but then she changed her mind again.

"Left? Yeah, left." He sprayed her left shoulder and patted it dry with a paper towel before transferring the stencil of the star onto her flesh. She gazed in a mirror. "How does it look? Should I move it lower before he starts?"

When the man took out a needle, I instinctively blurted out, "Is that sanitary? You're using a fresh needle, right?" I felt like I was channeling my father.

Not waiting for an answer, Lainie ordered, "Go ahead before I change my mind."

The man looked up at me as he put the needle on his tool. "Yup. It's safe. You think I'm nuts?"

"Well, yes," Gina muttered in my ear. "Doing this to a twelve-year-old."

I didn't want to sound like a parent, but I whispered for the last time, "Are you really, really sure?" My heart pounded so loud I could hear it thumping in my ears and feel it in my chest as he began. I held Lainie's hand to reassure her. And me.

Gina turned away as the tattoo artist pushed on a foot pedal about every ten seconds, outlining the five-pointed star. I remembered cutting myself with the razor when I shaved my legs. I imagined this was much worse, and started getting queasy. I placed my other hand on her chair for support. I thought I'd smell burning, but it was odorless. Sandy also held Lainie's hand as the man did a lot of wiping, which I figured was a good thing. My emotions were going out of control. One minute I thought we were all insane, letting her go through with this—we should have hog-tied her and whisked her away. The next I was in absolute awe that Lainie believed in something so much that she went after it with her whole heart without worrying about what we, her mother, or anyone else thought. It made me feel like a coward, because I hadn't ever taken a chance on anything that I truly wanted. I always felt as if I were waiting for something to happen. Like all these years wondering if Bobby sent me that love note, holding on to a crush. I wiped my palms, which were dripping with sweat. When the outline of her star was done, the man switched to another clean needle with a fatter tip and began to dip it into colored ink. At first I was nervous because the star looked blurry on her skin, and I had to bite my lower lip to keep from screaming, *Stop!*

"My pinky feels numb," Lainie said to the man.

"Sometimes there's referred pain in another part of the body. Don't worry." He continued to fill in the yellow color.

Gina looked worried. Sandy looked worried. I looked worried. Lainie was calm.

I leaned toward Gina. "And that's why *she's* having it done and *we're* not."

"No," said Gina, "she's having it done because she always needs to be in your face."

"Let's support her now," Sandy said. "Even if this wasn't the smartest thing to do."

Gina shrugged.

"Done." The man put down his tools and rubbed on A & D ointment.

"Already?" We all let out sighs of relief.

"Yeah." He covered the area on her shoulder with plastic wrap and then taped around it. "No bath. No sun for three days."

Sandy and I glanced over Lainie's shoulder—the one with the star now—and read the pamphlet he gave her: *Caring for the Wound.*

"Wound?" mouthed Sandy behind Lainie's back. "No sun? What about Florida?"

"How many days will it take to heal?" Lainie winced as she put on her jacket.

"Probably will feel fine by tomorrow. Tops, three days," said the man as he put away his tools.

"Can I shower?" she asked.

"Yeah," he told her. "Just keep it covered, like it says on that care sheet. Don't soak it."

As Lainie was about to close the door, she stuck her head back in. "Thanks."

"Good luck, kid. Come back if you want another one. You'd look sweet with a heart."

Lainie smiled, but her back stiffened when she put her bag over her shoulder.

"Does it hurt?" I asked. "You know my father works in a hospital if you need help."

"Yeah, it hurts, but I'm glad I did it. Now let's have lunch. I'm starved."

"I can't believe you could eat after that," I said, feeling nauseous.

As we left, we saw a pixie-like girl with coal-black hair

sprinkled with bright maroon highlights standing in a doorway. Her midriff-baring knit top revealed a silver navel ring. Lainie paused at the sign in the window, BODY PIERCING.

Gina pulled Lainie by the fur trim of her hooded jacket. "Keep walking."

"Is that what we're doing next?" Sandy giggled.

"*We?* You're on your own." Gina walked a few feet ahead. She dug her hands in her pockets and kicked a pebble with her boot. I had never seen her so quiet. I guess this was her way of not ragging on Lainie any more that day.

We caught up with Gina, grabbed some pizza, and followed Lainie around like lap dogs from store to store of vintage clothes. The four of us tried on so many clothes that it made the annual rummage sale at Gina's mom's church, Our Lady of Something (where she strategically collected sizes that no longer fit members of the parish after Thanksgiving), look absolutely bleak. In the end, we got the following for our first official boy-girl party:

Sandy

A black fifties-style flannel poodle skirt with a white dog on it, like in an old Elvis Presley beach-party flick. It had so many layers of crinoline under it, it made her look like a lampshade. (Luckily that look got old along with girdles and nylons with garter belts.) Black fishnet stockings were in again, so she got a pair of those—new, not the ripped ones in the bin that they were trying to pass off as "authentic." Lainie said, "It's okay to mix the fifties and sixties together in a funky, retro kind of thing you have going there, but chuck the saddle shoes and the anklets." She advised Sandy on the coolest-looking pair of red patent leather flats—shiny as a new penny. "They go better with your whole look. And you can dance in them," she added, tying a little polka-dot organza scarf around Sandy's neck for a final touch.

"You think anyone will ask me?" said Sandy.

Gina answered, "Why not? You look perfectly peachy," as Sandy twirled in front of a three-way mirror. Then Sandy started to hop around, doing old-fashioned dance movements. "*Now* you look like an idiot," Gina said.

Gina

The next victim was Gina. The only places she was halfway interested in were army-navy stores stacked with camouflage pants and khaki vests with lots of zippers and pockets.

"For fly-fishing?" asked Lainie. She gently knocked on Gina's head. "Hello, it's a party—like in festive. Boys. Makeup. Fun. Maybe go a little dressy for once?"

But Gina wouldn't budge. She bought secondhand beige cargo pants. "I'll dress them up with a red sweater," she conceded, to lessen Lainie's obvious disappointment in her lack of interest in fashion advice. Gina also had clearly fallen in love with a jacket, pulling it hastily off the rack as if someone else might grab it first.

"Promise me you won't wear that oversized, moth-eaten navy peacoat. You look like a docked sea captain." Lainie stared at the jacket with such disdain. "My dad left one of those in the attic when he split—genuine of the period. I'm certain he'd be willing to part with it for the evening. Particularly since he'll never know you wore it."

Gina mirrored Lainie's expression. "Thanks, but no thanks. I'm spending my last cent on this peacoat." I have to admit with the collar up she looked hip in that Gina kind of way of hers.

Lainie

Lainie, Lainie, Lainie, who I thought would be the most self-assured and buy something right on the spot, turned out to be exactly the opposite. She tried on so much, in so many places, the three of us nearly got eyestrain from rolling our eyes at each other. "You could wear a burlap potato sack with a rope around your waist, and it would become a bold fashion statement," Gina said.

After about twelve possibilities—even though she looked great in each and every one—Lainie chose a tight-fitting sea-foam cashmere sweater with a sequined scoop neck that showed off the rhinestone heart that always dangled, twinkling magically, between her angular collarbones. She found a pleated miniskirt with the silk lining ripped and a small stain near the hem.

Sandy said, "I'll help you sew it." Lainie was helpless in these things. She'd failed the home economics portion of our Life Cycles unit when she refused to master blind stitching (though the next month in woodworking shop she got an A using a lathe and heavy equipment to carve an intricate jewelry tray—greater motivation). Lainie took out her mother's American Express card (don't ask me how she got it) and threw in a pair of stud earrings that matched the color of her sweater.

Krista (me)

Now me. I'll start from the bottom up. Sandy got the urge for an egg roll in Chinatown. As we were walking downtown, we passed the Pearl River Trading Company in SoHo, and I found a pair of pine-green velvet ballet slippers real cheap. The soles looked like cardboard. Secondhand Rose had a matching green jacket with buttons that looped up to the neck of a mandarin collar. "It will look perfect with your jeans!" squealed Lainie. I also found a small bag embroidered with delicate gold threads, patterned like the many Chinese scrolls I had seen in my mother's art books. I smoothed my finger across the fine threads. "I'll buy it with my lunch money," I decided.

Sandy piped up, "I'll share my sandwich with you. I need to lose weight anyway before the party." Sweet, sweet Sandy.

"So do I," I said. "We'll lose together."

"You both look fine," Gina said, shooting us a look as we made our purchases.

Then we went to the lingerie store next door. While my friends were looking at accessories and trading elastic-beaded bracelets, I wandered over to the bras. There were padded, push-up, and strapless bras in all shapes, sizes, and colors. Some had cups large enough for honeydew melons. What was my size?

A woman sorting through some 38DDD's glanced up at me in a friendly way. "Can I help you?"

I backed away and stuttered, "N-n-no, I was just looking. Thank you." I scooped up a few that looked small and ran into a fitting room.

Sandy had once told me that Eric worked one summer at a big-name clothing store and said that there were surveillance cameras in dressing rooms hidden in walls and ceilings to prevent theft. My eyes searched every square inch of the space like a spy, and saw nothing. Even so, I slipped the bra on underneath my turtleneck sweater in case the mirror was two-way, like in those police dramas where there's a lineup and the victim has to identify the criminal on the other side of the wall. Since this was my first attempt, snapping the front closure was tough. But it was too small—I couldn't breathe. The next one had a catch in the back and I couldn't fasten it without twisting the bra around so that I could see what I was doing. The last—a pretty ivory one with a rosebud in the center—was for me. I dipped into my pocket to see how much money I had left.

There wasn't enough, so I took out the emergency money tucked in a compartment of my wallet and paid the woman at the register. Should I consider getting a bra an emergency? I felt like Goldilocks when she asked me how it fit and I answered, "Just right." She wrapped it in pale-pink tissue paper and smiled.

As I was putting it in my backpack, my friends asked me, "What did you get?"

I said the same thing I was going to say to my mother: "Oh, nothing."

Gina said, "Let me see." She snatched the bag the same way she had with Lainie's fake ID and pushed aside the tissue paper. "Oh." She handed it back to me, the 32A clearly visible on the tag.

Sandy blushed and Lainie put her arm on my shoulder and smiled.

I never thought I would appreciate Lainie getting a call from her mother as much as I did that very second. We could hear her screaming on the cell phone, "Where are you? It's almost dark!" as we headed quickly to the subway entrance.

All I could think was, which was bigger news—me getting a bra or Lainie getting a tattoo? For me, the answer was a no-brainer.

Fourteen

Daniel

Love, said Sophocles, is like the ice held in the hand by children.
A piece of ice held fast in the fist.
—Tom Stoppard, playwright

Krista looked flushed and hurried, carrying packages as she approached her house.

"Your mother's been waiting for you. It's late," Mr. Harris said to her.

"I was clothes shopping with my friends for a class party." She glanced over at me and my dad.

I decided I might as well break the news to my father. "I'm going too. It's at Bobby Kaufman's just before Christmas." You could have heard a pin drop.

My father's face tightened. "We'll talk about it later, Daniel."

Krista shot me one of those oh-boy-you're-in-deep-trouble looks.

When Dad came to pick me up after physical therapy was over, he slammed the car door when he got in and brusquely snapped the seat belt across his chest. "You're not going to that party. Do you understand?"

I didn't answer him, crossing my arms defensively as we headed home.

"Am I talking to thin air?"

I let out an obnoxious snort. Cold steam billowed from my breath.

"This is important to me. And to your mother."

"Do I see a mother here? And *this* is important to *me.*"

"Daniel Rosen . . ."

"Even if she's home by then, I'm going."

"I already got plane tickets to Louisiana as soon as your winter school vacation starts in December."

"You knew she wasn't coming home?" I shrugged. "So change them."

"They're nonrefundable. I can't."

"You can if you have a doctor's note. Say I'm still sick."

"But you're not." My father sounded flustered, like a three-year-old.

"I am, of listening to this. I don't care what you say. Go see your wife without me."

With that I headed into the house. My father followed, yelling after me, "You're being ridiculous. Go without you?" He looked hurt, like, *After all I've done for you.*

"And for the record, I couldn't care less about what *she* wants either."

"Oh, Daniel. *She?* It's your mother we're talking about."

"Don't 'oh, Daniel' me!" I glared right at him. "I hate her."

This time it was my turn to slam the door—to my bedroom, right in his face.

I saw line two of our telephone light up almost immediately. I picked up the receiver, held my breath as if I were under water—which I was an expert at—pressed the mute button, and listened.

"Hi, Emma, it's me."

"Oh, hi. How's it going? I can hardly wait to see you guys."

I could hear Dad let out a deep sigh full of so many unsaid words.

"What? What's the matter?" There was an urgency in my mother's voice.

"Nothing's wrong. Everyone's okay. Daniel's healthy."

Now it was my mother's turn to let out a deep sigh. "Then what?"

"Well . . ." He hesitated. "We're not going to be able to come after all. Sorry, Em."

"What do you mean? I've been making plans, getting brochures from places I wanted to take Daniel to. And there's a country-western band concert I'm in. Not a major deal, but still, I was looking forward to you seeing me fiddle in something so different."

"Not this time. Maybe you'll come home instead?"

There was silence. Then my mother said in a cold voice, "What's the problem, Bruce?"

Whenever my mother used my father's name I knew she was beyond angry. Most of the time she called him "Moose," because he was big and she liked to hug him and cuddle in his arms. He'd make blueberry pancakes for us on Sunday mornings or hot chocolate and popcorn with a DVD in the evening. We'd sit in a row like "three bugs in a rug," she would say. That was when they'd been happy—or when *she'd* been happy.

"There are a couple of problems, Em," Dad said. "First of all, this is no longer an extended vacation. Believe me, I understand a part of what you are doing. But the other part of me is starting to wonder, what's really going on here? This short little break is turning into a long separation."

Mom didn't answer.

"The next problem is it's Daniel's first co-ed party over winter break. After all we've all been through, if he wants to go and be a part of things, we should support him. Like before."

"Well, it's not 'like before,' in case you haven't noticed!" my mother snapped.

"I have something else to say." My father cleared his throat. "The party is at the Kaufmans'."

There was silence again for a few moments before my mother answered.

"You tell him for me that if he sets foot into that house, I don't know what I'll do." Her tone was seething.

I wanted to cry out, *Can't you be excited for me? This isn't about you!* But then they would know I had been eaves-dropping.

"Em, calm down," Dad said, then added firmly, "it's *his* choice. We need to stand by him."

With that, my mother did the same thing to my father that I had done to her. She hung up.

I could hear my father begin to cry as he put down the receiver. I hung up too. Was it my fault they had a fight? Or was it theirs? *I'm not going to feel guilty. I'm not going to feel guilty,* I repeated like one of my mother's mantras, over and over again in my mind. *I'm not going to feel guilty.* But I did. Great. Is this what I was going to have to get used to? Me being in between their stuff?

An hour later, there was a gentle knock at my bedroom door. "I made some dinner. Your favorite," my father said softly on the other side. "You must be hungry. I know I am. Come on, Dan. Open up."

I didn't answer, but when he finally went away, I heard my stomach grumble, so I opened my door and went into the kitchen. He was sitting in his chair. I sat down opposite him in mine. Mom's seat was empty—no plate of meatballs and spaghetti at her setting. We ate silently.

Before bedtime, I bumped into him in the bathroom, brushing his teeth. "I know you're feeling much better," he said around a mouthful of foam, looking like a rabid dog. "Because you're fighting for what you want."

I looked at him as if he were nuts. He tapped a framed sampler my mother had needlepointed during her Zen period when she was thinking of becoming a

Buddhist and we had to release ants and spiders outside in case we might come back as them in our next life. She'd hung it over the toilet so we'd see it every day. It had become part of the background and I rarely noticed it anymore, except the time I'd smashed a bug on the glass with a tissue and felt guilty for a week wondering, *What if that was Grandpa?*

> *The rocks are where they are—this is their will.*
> *The rivers flow—this is their will.*
> *The birds fly—this is their will.*
> *Human beings talk—this is their will.*
> *The seasons change, heaven sends down rain or snow,*
> *The earth occasionally shakes,*
> *The waves roll, the stars shine—*
> *Each of them follows its own will.*
> *To be is to will and so is to become.*

I would have preferred to hang a Far Side cartoon I'd once seen: *I wish you much joyful weirdness in your lives.* That would be a better mantra for Mom.

Over Thanksgiving weekend, I watched my father work and the tadpole dodge pebbles—both going nowhere. It was so boring I went online and wrote on the class blog: *The tadpole's getting a mysterious frontal body swelling. If anyone's out there, what is the diagnosis?*

Krista must have been looking at it too, because she sent me an instant message: *Can I come over?*

I zipped back: *Yes.*

"I hope it's not dying of some rare disease," she said, out of breath. She whipped off her woolen scarf and hat and rushed into the kitchen with me. "Like warts from humans."

"Sure, Krista," I said, shaking my head. "I think the myth is the other way around."

We peered into the tank. The tadpole remained on its belly. "Is it resting?" She tapped the tank. "Maybe it's saving up energy for a growth spurt. People often stop growing before they start and really take off." She smiled. "See the itsy bumps up front? I think it's a good sign."

"So," I said with a sigh of relief, "want anything to drink? To celebrate new legs."

She let out a laugh and shrugged. "Sure, why not. To fresh frog's legs."

I looked inside the cabinets. Since my mother left, Dad had stopped buying herbal tea. There was no baker's chocolate for melting, or dark cocoa, or even an instant mix with tiny marshmallows. Then I saw a half-gallon of apple cider on a shelf in the back of the refrigerator. It hadn't reached its expiration date yet, so I poured some into two mugs and nuked them. I added a stick of cinnamon I found in one of Mom's Ball jars that she kept over the stove, and handed one to Krista. The steam curled Krista's bangs into frizz on her forehead.

"This smells so good." She swirled the stick in the mug, taking in the sweet aroma.

We sipped silently. A perfect round moon formed in

the sky. We craned our necks as we stared out the window, trying to see it clearly over the large oak tree in the backyard. "Do you want to see it better?" I asked. Krista nodded. She put on her hat and mittens, wrapping the long scarf around her like a mummy. Then she followed me to a wooden swing hanging from a thick branch in our yard and sat down next to me. Three brilliant stars glimmered in a row. "See Orion's belt?" I pointed to the sky.

She arched her back to follow the direction of my finger. "Yes, I see them!"

"And there's Gemini—the twins." I thought to myself, *Like we used to be.*

"This is beautiful. I see them too!"

"Some other stars travel in pairs. They're called binary stars. They're a balancing force, locked in an embrace, pulling on each other around an imagined point. Sometimes there are black holes in binary systems. A black hole is what an old star turns into when it dies. Even though a black hole is a dead star, it still tugs on its stellar companion. Bodies of stars can orbit a black hole. When I was in the hospital, my mother made me a stargazer. She cut stencils of the constellations and projected them onto the ceiling of my room—like in the planetarium. We spent hours watching our own private star show as we listened to jazz or her violin pieces. She brought the heavens inside."

"Wow. It's just like your mother to think of something like that." Krista gave a wistful sigh.

"Every night I went to sleep knowing that the following

one I could always count on my mother, and always a starry sky."

"If there's rain, the stars are still there; they don't disappear. You just can't see them at the moment. Everything comes back in time. You know that, Daniel."

"That's so Buddhist of you," I teased her. "My mother would like that."

Krista smiled and said nothing as we stared at the blanket of stars. Instead of the pitch-black night being scary, it seemed peaceful sitting next to her. My mother was a real magician to think of something so wonderful as a stargazer. *So why would a person like that leave? Why can't she make magic at home?* I wished on a twinkling star she'd come back. For me.

Fifteen

Krista

At every step you will have to decide who you are.
And who you are will change.
—Lee Blessing, playwright

My mother saw me moping around the house all weekend and said her usual, "What's up?"

And I said my usual, "Nothing," which meant: *Leave*
me alone; mind your own business.

"Did you call a friend?"

"They're away," I pouted. "Did you forget? I told you
already. No one's home!"

"What about Daniel?"

"What about him?" I said, feeling more annoyed.
"Am I his keeper?"

I didn't tell her I already had seen him. That we
watched stars shift and twinkle in his backyard. That *I*
went to *him.* And we talked like when we were best
friends. But now that we were older, something felt different. My heart wasn't as open as a six- or seven-year-
old's—I wasn't like soft, mushy Matt, who hugged and

kissed and cried whenever and wherever and to whomever he wanted without that whole layer of protection like a thick banana skin. I didn't tell her I bought my first bra. Or that Lainie got a tattoo. And that I was never alone with Bobby like I was with Daniel, so how could I know that I even liked him as a person?

She wouldn't get out of my face—parents do that if you don't feed them some tidbit of information when you're moody. I made a regular history assignment seem like a bigger deal than it was—even though, truth be told, it would never get me bent out of shape. "Our entire grade is studying Egypt. Each of us has to do some kind of project, and I am going to fail if I can't figure out what I should do—other than embalming Matt with his rock collection and then doing an archeological dig in our backyard months later."

My mother shook her head, then walked over to the bookshelves in our living room and opened one of her old art history books from college. "The pyramids look as if they're in the middle of a vast desert, but if you see them in person, they could be anywhere in Queens. There's even a McDonald's on the way to the ones near Cairo."

"Gee, Ma, thanks for sharing that, in case I wasn't depressed enough."

She gave me her I-knew-something-was-up expression.

"Get dressed, hon. We're going to the Metropolitan Museum of Art."

Mom brought orange juice and bagels, which we ate on the express bus into the city. The driver let us off near the entrance. We headed directly for the gift shop on the main floor, and went upstairs to the children's books and toys. That's the other side of my mother—the side I liked. Things didn't have to be in order—like they were on class trips, where we always went to a gift shop at the end of the day, after I could barely move and was museumed out. I got a piece of paper made out of papyrus from the Nile River and a cheap bookmark with hieroglyphics on it for Matt. "He would prefer a sarcophagus," I told Mom as we headed for the Temple of Dendur in the Egyptian wing, "but this will have to do."

We saw every exhibit in the hall, except when my mother got claustrophobic as we came to the end of a tight passageway in a tomb crowded with a group of tourists. She tugged at her turtleneck sweater, pulling it away from her throat, and held on to a rail beside a glass wall protecting the ancient, carved stone.

"Are you okay, Ma?" I asked as she led us away to get something to drink.

"I'm fine, sweetheart." She wiped perspiration from her brow.

We took out a map of the museum and walked to the great dining hall.

"When I was younger, Grandma used to take me for morning art lessons at the junior museum downstairs. Then we'd go for lunch in the cafeteria. I'd have a hamburger with kosher dill pickle chips and we'd share one French cruller. Once in a while, we'd go to the fancy dining room upstairs off the main gallery. There was an enormous meditation pool in the center with Greek statues, and seating all around with skylights above." She closed her eyes. "I can still hear the clinking silverware." I stared at the center of room—the pool gone, now filled with noisy people clanging dishes and scarfing down their food. "We'd sit at a table near the edge of the water, and I'd toss a penny in among the others and make a wish."

"Do you remember what that wish was?"

She drew in a breath. "To become a famous artist like one in the museum."

"You became an art teacher. You're famous in your school. You like that, don't you?"

My mother didn't answer me. Her deep sigh said a lot. "Or probably the wish was something silly." She sipped her lemon tea. "Like hoping Frances Kellerman became flat as a knock hockey board overnight and that David Lloyd Fisher got fleas from her sheepdog."

I looked down at my hot turkey platter, as if I hadn't had enough turkey on Thanksgiving Day, and pierced the peas with my fork, pushing them aimlessly in the gravy.

"Sweetheart." She reached over and stroked my fingers. "I didn't mean to say thinking about a boy is silly. It's just as you get older, things become more complex." Tears pooled in my eyes until they ran down my cheeks onto my mashed potatoes. Her warm hand remained on mine. "Oh, honey, what's the matter?"

I couldn't tell her how confused I was about Bobby, Daniel, and me. About growing up.

Then, ever so softly, she said, "This is a poem called

'Brown Penny' by William Butler Yeats. I had to memorize it in high school. I think it goes . . ."

> I whispered, "I am too young,"
> And then, "I am old enough";
> Wherefore I threw a penny
> To find out if I might love.

"The last half of the first stanza is muddled in my brain, but I remember the last one."

> O love is the crooked thing,
> There is nobody wise enough
> To find out all that is in it,
> For he would be thinking of love
> Till the stars had run away,
> And the shadows eaten the moon.
> Ah, penny, brown penny, brown penny,
> One cannot begin it too soon.

"I guess things aren't simple at your age either. If only I could make life easier for you and soak up all your sorrows with a sponge." She squeezed my hand. "But then how would you learn to weather and balance the ups and downs?" I looked into her gray-brown eyes, and for some odd reason we began to giggle. My mother took her napkin and dabbed my cheeks. "Romantic love can get kind of sappy, like the poem. In a wonderfully deep sort of way. And you're never too young to feel love. I love you, Krista."

"I love you too, Mom."

By the time we left the museum it was getting dark. We walked out the entrance down the steep steps past a man selling hot chestnuts and warm, salted pretzels from a cart. Fountains gushed in a long shallow pool sprinkling ribbons of mist in tiny spotlights surrounding the water. Mom unzipped her pocketbook and handed me a shiny penny. "Make a wish."

Should I wish that Bobby suddenly realized it was *me* he liked? And Gina would not even think to say "BK and LM" in a tattoo heart? That Daniel could walk and swim alone? That I looked like Lainie, acted like Sandy, and had Gina's strength? What did I really want for me? I closed my eyes, then opened them. "Can I postpone a wish?"

She folded her fingers around the penny, pressing it in my palm. "It's your wish. You can do anything you want." This time, I closed my eyes tighter, then flung the penny into the water. When I opened them, the moon rose like a copper coin in the sky above Central Park behind the glass atrium of the museum. My mother pulled mittens over my hands. "Don't tell anyone if you want it to come true."

When we got home, Dad and Matt were playing Go Fish, and Matt had a bigger pile of cards. Maybe my father was letting him win. We ordered Chinese food. While we waited for the order to come, my mother's eyes suddenly lit up like they did when she had one of her teacher-brainstorming sessions. I hoped it wouldn't be like the time Matt and I were guinea pigs for plaster face masks and I couldn't smile comfortably for twenty-four hours—although it did dry up a humongous pimple.

She lined the ingredients on the Formica countertop like a short-order cook.

"Get me some baking soda, sweetie," she asked Matt as she salted a chicken.

"Yuck! I'm not eating that!" Matt hollered.

"No one's asking you to." When we brought the soda, she added it and rubbed the entire outside of the chicken with olive oil. "Rip these into thin long strips," she demanded, handing Dad one of my old striped pillowcases from the rag bin near the washing machine. When Dad was done, she began to wrap the chicken in cloth. "All right, Krista, now you finish up," she instructed, "like this."

I turned to Matt as I continued to encase the thighs and wings. "I think she's lost it. We should restrain her with these strips." I was totally mystified. "What *are* we doing?"

My father laughed, reminding me, "Hey, budding scientist, remember when you won the science fair growing crystals for your snowflake project? Or when you carbonized wood into charcoal and Grandpa gave you his seltzer cartridge to demonstrate refrigeration?"

"Now a spritz!" Mom sprayed the chicken with water like Sandy squirted herself with her mother's good French perfume. "In twenty days, we'll dump everything and embalm it again, and in forty days it will be mummified!"

"You're turning a chicken into a mummy?" I rolled my eyes.

Matt stuck out his arms and bumped into the kitchen chairs and table. He deepened his squeaky voice. "The revenge of the mummy's curse!"

"Which mummy do you mean?" I looked from my mother to the raw chicken. "It looks like an orthopedic patient at a veterinary hospital. Or your papier-mâché mask."

My mother batted my arm gently.

I twirled around. "Sometimes you surprise me, Ma. So that's my project?"

She whisked stray hairs away from her face. Specks of baking soda flecked her cheeks and the hand-stitched apron I had made for her in fifth grade. "Sometimes I surprise myself."

"Thanks, Mom, for turning a boring history assignment into a wonderful science one—my favorite subject in the entire world." I placed my messy hands around her neck.

My mother smiled. Dad put on the new Norah Jones CD, then put out his hand to Mom and began to dance with her. Matt and I watched them and squeezed in, like two pieces of salami between their slices of bread. The four of us swayed in the center of the kitchen.

"Okay," she said when the song was over, "time to clean up."

My parents remained in each other's arms for a few extra seconds.

Sunday evening was a perfect finish to a perfect day.

My friends came home. I logged on to AIM and they were all online.

> **Freckleface:** I'm b-a-a-c-k! I loved Boston—like out of a science fiction movie. Looks like the entire population over thirty was wiped out. Eric's now applying to colleges mostly there.

> **TuttiFrutti:** My uncle made an offer on an Ice King business in Cape May, which my dad might invest in. Will that make me an Ice Princess?

> **Headshot:** Died and went to heaven. Hotel lobby had flowing curtains, no doors, candelabras, a marble sushi bar, dramatic lighting—a dreamlike stage set like *Phantom of the Opera*. And everything was white: the pool chaise lounges, the fluffy pillows, the hotel rooms. *Everyone* was there.

> **TuttiFrutti:** Everyone? Like whom?

> **Headshot:** Important people.

> **Biobuff:** Hey, aren't we important anymore?

Sixteen

Daniel

The world is a fine place and worth fighting for.
—Ernest Hemingway, author

Lunchtime was way above freezing, which meant basketball on the blacktop. Gina scored basket after basket while Brandon cried out each time she shot, "I can do better than that!"

"In your dreams!" she shouted back.

"In yours!" he yelled, demanding a rematch after school.

"You're on!" Gina cried out. "Today at three-thirty. My house. And I've got a ball."

"If you want to come, Daniel," Lainie offered, "I'll forge a note from your father so the driver of your van will let you off in front of Gina's house after school instead of yours. She's the only girl on our block with a brand-new basketball hoop."

"And Lainie's a pro at making things fake," Gina put in. Lainie made a face at her.

Like a duel or a shoot-out in the Old West, a bunch of us showed up on Twenty-fifth Avenue for a playoff between Brandon and Gina, and boys against girls. I don't know if it was because we were invited to Bobby's party, but this felt like a trial run of getting together. Gina's grandmother was poised on the front porch near the driveway trying to feed everyone pignoli cookies as they showed up to form two teams. "All this running around, you'll need strength!" She came over, holding a plate out to me. "Look at you. A string bean. You're like vermicelli. Doesn't your mama feed you? You're a growing boy."

I gave her a polite smile, glancing down at my worn sneakers, the soles beginning to split near my big toes. My mother would have noticed them pushing through and made sure to buy me new ones at the mall.

Bobby waved me over, dribbling the ball back and forth in front of me and around me, and finally handing it over. "Shoot!"

I stood fixed.

"Pretend I'm Coach."

"Thanks, but no thanks. You're not Coach."

"Come on, Rosen," he persisted. "Just do it."

I looked at everyone waiting for me to shoot the basket. "This isn't a Nike ad."

Bobby didn't back off. I braced myself against the bar of my walker and aimed for the hoop, both arms outright. The ball bounced on the rim and missed.

"Do over!" hollered Gina. "It's my house, I can call it."

The second shot swished through the net. Gina put two fingers in her mouth and gave one of those shrill whistles as everyone slapped me on the back—everyone except Krista. I glanced over at her, and she looked away. And I wondered, *Why?*

Lainie, looking fit and tan, went on and on between plays about the commercial she did over Thanksgiving as we tried to concentrate on the game. She tripped on the corner of my walker. Gina muttered under her breath as some members of the boys' team helped her up, "There goes Snow White and the Seven Dorks." Lainie stayed out the rest of the game on the sidelines with Nonna, showing her pictures from the commercial instead of watching Bobby, Brandon, Jeremy, Harry, and me taking turns getting slaughtered.

Sandy kept repeating, "Whoa! I don't believe it!"

"Believe it!" Gina wiped her brow with her sleeve. "We deserve to win."

And they did. Gina gave Krista and Sandy a high five, and the three of them jumped in a circle together as one. Lainie slowly walked over to congratulate them. Their arms remained linked without her, and she said in this really sweet voice—almost too sweet, brushing her arm against Bobby's—"Basketball's not really my thing. Did you see my glossies?" And she flipped through some photos of her by the ocean and pool with palm trees in the background. Krista's expression turned from a smile to not quite a frown.

Nonna invited everyone for homemade pizza. "I got

two kinds: Sicilian and regular. Anyone would have to have brains as soft as cannolis to turn down my pies," she insisted. We gave each other looks, like, should we go inside? But Nonna grabbed my wrist and led me by the arm. "I'm going to stuff you like a manicotti."

The only sound was us chewing as we sat around the large kitchen table. Lainie dabbed at the oil on her slice with a napkin and scraped off most of the cheese before she took a small bite, leaving it oozing in a puddle on her plate like lava.

"Does this count as a pizza party for Daniel?" I overheard Sandy whisper.

Krista shot her a look and shook her head.

What did they mean?

After we were done stuffing our faces, Gina's uncle Carmine dropped me off at my house on the way to his store.

"Where were you?" my father grilled me at the front door, pacing like a lion.

"What are you, a warden?"

"What are you talking about? I'm your father. You think this is a prison?"

"Right now I do."

"Daniel. You have to call. So I know you're safe."

"You could have called the bus company, and the driver would have told you where I was dropped off. Mom would have known to do that."

"Well, your mother isn't here. *I am.* Get used to it. I have to know where you are."

"I used to hang out after school! Skateboarding!" I slammed the door to my bedroom.

And my father slammed his.

"Is this what I'm going to have to get used to?" I screamed through the closed door.

An hour later I heard my Dad on the other side. "Daniel?"

I ignored him.

"Daniel, this isn't right. Us fighting like this."

I put the pillow over my ears and began to hum softly to myself.

"Can I come in?" he insisted.

Before the accident, I would have pushed at the door with all my strength to prevent him from entering, but now how could I?

I stopped humming when he stood at the foot of my bed. "This isn't about the accident, Daniel. You're my child and I need to know where you are at all times. You're not a grown-up yet."

I said nothing.

He sat on my bed and moved the pillow away. "You've got to understand. This is out of love. It's not a control thing." Then he glanced down at my ratty sneakers on the floor. "I thought we'd go out for a bite, do a little shopping." I shrugged. He handed me my sneakers and untied the frayed edges of the laces before I began to put them on grudgingly.

"I can do it," I said with an edge.

"I know you can." He looked up into my eyes and gave a slight smile. "So can I."

When we got to the mall and passed a shoe store, my father paused in front of the display of the new Adidases and other brands. "Pick out a new pair."

"You sure?" I asked, looking over at a boy shopping with his mother.

"Are you kidding?" Dad bent over and pinched my sock where it protruded from my sneaker. "You've got air-conditioning."

The sales clerk asked, "Do you want to wear them? I'll box the old ones."

Dad answered, "The only thing those are good for is the garbage." And he added as we left, "You need a pair of jeans too. I know the exposed knee is sometimes in, but this look has stepped over the line of being cool. And how about a new shirt or two? When was the last time you went shopping? You're going to a party in a few weeks." He tousled my hair.

We hugged each other, and I didn't care who in the mall saw us.

Seventeen

Krista

The future is built on brains, not prom court,
as most people will tell you after
attending their high school reunion.
—Anna Quindlen, columnist and novelist

Sandy brought over pale green eye shadow to go with my Chinese jacket and shoes. While she brushed some powder on my eyelids and dabbed our cheekbones with the body glitter Lainie had loaned her, Matt barged into my bedroom. "I knew I should have gotten dressed at your house!" I said to Sandy. "At least *your* brother respects privacy!" Then I remembered Eric staring at me through Sandy's bedroom window. "Okay, what?" I said to Matt. "What's so important that it can't wait until tomorrow?"

Matt glanced up at me, unfolded his chubby fingers like a petal slowly opening, and shared the gift in the palm of his hand. "Maybe you'd like to put this on for the party?"

I picked up a paste-on tattoo of a little bug-eyed frog. Sandy began to smile, and it made me smile too.

"I thought you'd like it since you have a tadpole in your classroom."

I bent down. "Oh, Matt, it's so cute. And the frog's almost the same green as my jacket."

He watched Sandy rub it on the same spot as Lainie's. "At least this comes off by tomorrow," she whispered.

"Try by tonight," I whispered back as Matt left, looking proud and useful.

Gina called twice to ask, "Are you guys ready yet?" The third time, she blurted out, "I'm going through puberty waiting here."

Lainie must have called a trillion times. I had lost count.

Sandy brought out her mom's good perfume. "You never know."

"Sandy!" I jabbed her in the arm.

"Don't 'Sandy' me." She lifted my hair and gave me a playful squirt on my neck.

We hugged each other, then walked into the living room. My father blinded us taking snapshots. *"Dad!"* I screamed.

"I'm going to download these babies instantly," said my mother, "and e-mail them to Grandma in Boca. Wait till she shows these pictures around the condo club."

"Next time, my house." Sandy smiled politely.

"You're telling me. My family's out of control. I can imagine what'll happen if I get married someday."

"If?" repeated my mother without missing a beat. "What do you mean *if* you get married someday?"

"Ma! Leave me alone. I'm going to be a scientist or a doctor. Not a wife."

Sandy gave me a thumbs-up sign.

"Parents!" I rolled my eyes.

"What?" My father elbowed my mother in the side. "What did we do?"

My mother leaned over as we put on our coats to go across the street to Lainie's. She gave me a big kiss on the forehead and said in my ear, "If you want, you can have it all, honey: doctor, wife, mother. Now have a wonderful time tonight."

When Lainie answered the door, her mother was right behind her, flicking an eyelash off Lainie's cheek and carefully patting her hair in place. "Not too late."

Lainie whisked her hand away, trying to fluff it out. "Ma, it was fine the way it was."

The three of us smiled awkwardly, left, and went down the block to get Gina.

"Tonight feels like late autumn, not winter," said Lainie, shaking out her long locks.

An inflated snowman lit up the Delucas' front lawn in the center of two life-sized blinking reindeer, reminding us Christmas was just a few days away. A wreath rattled as Nonna opened the screen door, left on from the summer. She repeated to each of us, *"Bellissima. Molto bella!"* Gina came downstairs in her cargo pants and threw on the peacoat. Nonna raised both hands toward the roof.

"What?" asked Gina impatiently.

"This is how a person goes to a party? You couldn't wear something nicer?"

Gina glared at my green Chinese jacket. "You mean like her?"

"Okay, if that's how you want to go, but to me, you look like you're enlisting."

Gina pushed us out the front door and down the porch stoop to the sidewalk as Nonna saluted her like an admiral. "Love you too, Nonna. *Ciao!*" she mumbled. "I can hardly wait until I drive and can leave here without the Inquisition."

"Wasn't that Spanish, not Italian?" Lainie quipped.

Gina gave her one of her looks. As we approached the block, a few boys and girls were being dropped off by their parents or in carpools. Lainie searched her purse, found some lip gloss, and reapplied it generously. "We'll be fashionably late."

"Do I look okay?" I whispered to Sandy.

Sandy nodded. "Stop worrying."

Suddenly I felt a tug toward home. What if there was dancing and no one asked me, and I was the only girl standing alone? Or if there was Spin the Bottle like at camp last year during the cast party after the end-of-the-summer play? My group of friends were the only ones who hadn't really kissed yet. My stomach began to do flips, and I got so nervous I began to perspire. Great. Now I was going to smell like moldy-oldy Jeremy. A chill came over me as we passed through silver streamers hung over the door to the basement. Music blasted. A string of tiny turquoise lights flashed in rhythm. An eerie

purple bulb dangled from the ceiling, making everything white glow fluorescent in the dark: the paper stars
and moons that rotated gently, the Styrofoam icicles, and
especially Daniel's new tennis sneakers. Sandy squeezed
my hand. Hers was damp and clammy. I could feel her
excitement and knew I wasn't alone.

Some of the boys were munching on a large bowl of
chips, double-dipping into the salsa, and picking through
CDs with their greasy fingers. Brandon wore goofy black
eyeglasses with a big pink plastic nose and thick black
mustache attached to the frame. He lifted his disguise
each time he grabbed a nacho, which he used as a shovel
to scoop drippy cheddar cheese into his mouth. When
he came over, he wiggled his eyebrows and pretended to
flick ashes into the air from his large brown cigar, still in
its cellophane wrapper. "So, little ladies, you come here
often?" he began in his best Groucho Marx voice.

Gina snapped his bow tie. "Beat it before that cigar
learns division."

Brandon stuck his chest out like a puffin. "So you
think you're a tough guy," he said, sounding like a gang-
ster from one of those old black-and-white detective
movies.

"Gina's just tough on the outside." I smiled at her.

She looked at me with a bemused expression, narrow-
ing her eyes. That's when I saw Bobby over her shoulder,
swigging root beer from a bottle. My heart stopped. He
was wearing dark jeans with a black sweater, his sleeves
pushed up just enough. He moved to the beat of the

music, and with each downbeat, he did this little sway with his hips. The bass was turned way up on the speakers and I couldn't even hear myself breathe. Behind him, Daniel was waving to me from the couch. He was now seated next to the pile of jackets, heaped high as a mountain. When Bobby turned around to lower the sound on the CD player, I waved back. I wondered how Daniel got down that flight of steps to the basement. Did his father carry him? I would die. Did Mr. Kaufman help him? Worse. What did they say to each other if he did? Or did Bobby's parents even know Daniel was here?

Mrs. Kaufman turned on the overhead light, glanced halfway down the stairs, and gave a little smile. "Have a good time!" she shouted, which was probably her way of saying without saying, *I'm upstairs if there's any funny business.*

Bobby turned the dimmer down as soon as she left. As we all danced in the semidarkness, I couldn't help but wonder what must be going through Daniel's mind. When the song was over, the girls remained on one side of the room seated in a row on folding chairs near the wall unit, and the boys hung out on the other, next to the soda and snacks. There was another song, this time a slow one, and no one danced. By the third it got weird—the only thing moving in the center of the room was Bobby's dog, Max, slobbering over stray bits of potato chips and pretzel nuggets that had made their way from under the table to the dance floor. Hardly anyone was talking, until after Harry threw an ice cube down Jeremy's hooded sweatshirt, and Jeremy tried to get him back by mashing a cube in his mouth and then dribbling the crushed ice onto Harry's head as he held him in a firm headlock.

"This is the most fun I've had," Gina whined, "since I watched Nonna get her mole removed."

"And I haven't had such an exciting time since I witnessed Matt picking lint from his belly button and eating it," I said as Bobby made Jeremy release Harry by putting Jeremy in a headlock.

"Come on. Brandon's now singing karaoke and he can't lip-synch to save his life. Just what I want to see—some white boy doing rap, acting like he's in the hood instead of a wood-paneled playroom in Queens." Gina jutted her chin in Brandon's direction. "Yo, B man! Your pants are so low I can see the snowmen on your boxers." Brandon hiked up his pants and belted them tighter.

Bobby turned up the amp to his electric guitar and fiercely strummed several chords as Brandon returned to singing. I couldn't make out the lyrics. There was a bang on the ceiling, like a broom or something, and he stopped. After a minute Bobby started picking at the steel strings again, and a light to the basement was flicked on and off several times to get his attention.

"Yeah?" he yelled upstairs.

"I'd like to remain in this neighborhood," called an anonymous voice from the top of the stairs that resembled his mother's, "without a visit from the police."

Bobby tried a different guitar this time, with nylon strings, attached to a mike. His father hollered, "Keep it down." The white acoustical-tiled ceiling vibrated as we heard footsteps retreating on squeaky floorboards to another part of the house. In surrender?

Bobby put his instruments away while Brandon passed around a big black top hat that a magician would wear with each of our names scribbled on a slip of paper inside.

"Guess he came with a whole bag of tricks," Gina quipped.

"Each girl take a blue piece of paper with a boy's name on it. Now go stand next to the boy. Each boy should take a pink piece with a girl's name. Next dance, boys go find their girls," Brandon explained.

Gina started to move away as the hat came toward us, but I pulled on her sleeve and handed her one of the slips.

"Thanks a lot," she mouthed. "I'm going to kill you."

At first no one moved, ignoring Brandon's orders. Then, slowly, the girls wove in and out of the pack of boys. Gina stood in front of Brandon. She looked as if someone had asked her to eat a giant slug. Sandy got Harry, who was popping breath mints.

"Hope he doesn't try and kiss you, because your braces might lock," Lainie said.

Sandy gave her a whack on the arm.

Daniel's name was on my slip. I had hoped for Bobby. Disappointed, I walked over and sat next to him on the couch. Then I looked up. Lainie stood in front of Bobby. Someone turned on the music. They moved closer. Her hand went on his shoulder. His, on the small of her back. Once again, my heart stopped, but this time it was different. It ached.

"Do you want to go outside?" Daniel asked. "The sky is so clear tonight."

I glanced over at Lainie and Bobby again. "Sure, it's stuffy in here."

I opened the sliding glass door to the backyard. The cutoff tennis balls covering the bottom back legs of Daniel's walker got stuck on the aluminum track and wouldn't budge.

"This is how I came in earlier. Nothing happened then."

I got on my hands and knees, trying to glide the wedged wheels over the hump. When I finally did it, we went up the slate path toward the brick patio.

"Hey, we're getting a draft in here!" someone cried out, slamming the door shut.

Daniel didn't have a choice about not being included in dancing. Right now, neither did I. A slip of paper chose that for me. And it made me sad that I felt that way—even sadder than being left out of the dancing. Paper luminaria bags filled with sand and a flickering candle in each bag lined a path around the patio. Snowflakes perched between bushes were scattered in mulched flowerbeds around the plastic-covered inground pool that almost filled the entire yard. Pop-rock dance music blared in the distance. Daniel leaned slightly toward me and got this look in his eye as if he was going to kiss me. I wasn't sure how I felt. Then the music stopped.

I was startled when I suddenly felt a tap on my shoulder. "I was looking for you."

Bobby stood by my side. "For me?" A shiver went down my spine.

He shoved a pink slip of paper with my name on it in front of my face.

"Oh." I turned toward Daniel. "You'll be okay?"

"Why wouldn't I?" Daniel answered without looking at me, staring up at the sky.

"Okay then." I shuffled away.

Slow music started. The air felt close. A bead of sweat dripped down my stomach. Bobby's palm was moist in mine. He fumbled with his other hand near my waist. It felt heavy, like a lead weight. We stood a good distance apart—much farther than he and Lainie had. We moved from side to side, our legs stiff and wooden as he moved his way and I moved mine. He and Lainie had been in rhythm. It seemed so easy and natural for them. Not us. The whole thing caught me off guard. Suddenly bright lights went on. I froze. Brandon and Lainie were standing by the switch, giggling as Brandon made kissing sounds, smacking his lips together.

Bobby left me in the middle of the dance floor and went over to him. "Hey, Wiseguy."

I was alone. Standing there. Embarrassed and feeling horrible.

The song came to an end and Brandon shouted, "Change partners!"

Just when I thought things couldn't get any worse, Brandon snapped the back of Gina's bra like a bow and arrow. Thank God he didn't know I was wearing mine for the first time. I felt as if everyone knew. She spun around, clenching her fist. "You think you're Robin Hood? You try that again and you'll be singing like Friar Tuck." Gina turned to me. "I'm outta here."

"The four of us should go home together," I suggested. "Or one of our parents should pick us up."

"I don't want to be in the same room with him, let alone on the same planet. I doubt we're even members of the same species."

She walked over to Sandy and Daniel, who were joking around together. Sandy was sort of dancing with him as he rolled to the music. I should have thought of that instead of always thinking of myself and Bobby. Gina joined them, and then Harry. They made up their own dance moves.

Lainie and Bobby began singing along to Bobby's parents' old *Rubber Soul* Beatles album. Everyone joined in when John Lennon and Paul McCartney began the cut of "It's Only Love." Bobby slipped his fingers through Lainie's. I couldn't sing. I wanted to disappear. Then the lights went off completely. That's when I left.

I wanted to get away from watching them. Away from the music in my ears, the words of love in my brain. Away from my thoughts. I rushed into the bathroom and locked the door. It reeked of smoke. A cigar butt was in a plastic cup half filled with Coke. Dumb Brandon. I flushed it down the toilet and then leaned over the sink, feeling nauseous. I splashed cold water on my eyes to wash away the sting of my tears and stared into the mirror. *You stupid, stupid fool, Krista. Didn't you see what was in front of you? Or didn't you want to? Who's the dumb one now?*

I wiped my puffy eyes on the part of the towel that wasn't smeared with pizza stains and unlocked the door. When I opened it, getting on my I'm-okay face, determined to act as if nothing had happened, Daniel was waiting outside. "There's cake over there if you want some. Chocolate fudge, your favorite." *Oh, Daniel, you know my favorite.*

I looked over for a split second and leaned against the wall for support. They were still holding hands. I felt like Matt's panda bear, when the stuffing had been knocked out of it and he dragged it around for weeks with only its outside fur intact. "No thanks."

"Are you sick?" Daniel stood next to me, sipping soda. He handed me his cup. "I learned to share in preschool." Before I could say no, I took a sip. It felt cool going down the back of my throat, which was raw from gagging and crying.

"You were always a pretty good sharer." I tried to smile. "Even in kindergarten," I added.

"Even in third grade."

"What do you mean?" I stared straight at him.

"Remember Valentine's Day? That box of candy I gave you was big enough for the entire class."

I gave him a blank expression. Inside, I was on fire.

"The one from Bobby's grandfather's store," he went on, but I could barely listen to the words. "I saved my allowance for a whole four months to get you the double-layer one."

The candy wasn't from Bobby? Bobby didn't write the love note? Daniel did? Daniel and I had become two stars circling around a common center: Bobby. Had Bobby become my black hole? My one big gravitational pull? A star that had died.

I was crushed. I wanted to rush home and crawl under the covers. "I don't know what you're talking about." That was all I could say.

He looked at me with such a hurt expression. "You don't remember, Krista?"

"Remember what?"

And then on the other side of the room Bobby kissed Lainie. A long soul kiss.

And Lainie felt what I was supposed to feel tonight.

What I had been waiting for.

Some adults think you're just a kid, what do you know about that stuff? What do you know about wanting to be kissed and feeling warm down so deep it goes through your bones? About wanting that kiss so badly it physically aches if you don't have it? But I do.

Now I knew a little more about Daniel's suffering. How love and anger and hope can get confused, and in the blink of an eye things can change forever and break your heart wide open.

Eighteen

Daniel

We may as well dream of the world as it ought to be.
—Toni Morrison, author

Krista was lying. I couldn't believe she didn't remember that valentine box. One that size is hard to forget. It's like an elephant in the room. When I said the words "that box of candy I gave you," the one word "I" did me in. She looked at me as if I were dirt. I could see from her face she thought it was from someone else—like Bobby, from the way she stared at him. I had wondered why she never sent back an answer to the love note. Now she knows the truth. Kidding herself would be worse. It's like a Band-Aid you're afraid to rip off but know you have to in one fast tear so you can expose the wound to the air and finally let it heal.

The party wound down in an endless wave of dancing as Brandon DJed the songs, and Bobby and Lainie made out in the corner behind a potted rubber plant. As we waited on the driveway like little kids for carpool, my father and Mr. Harris arrived at the same time. They parked by the curb and got out. Dr. Kaufman walked across the lawn, his arm extended. He shook Krista's dad's hand first and then my father's. There was no "I'm sorry." Instead, just a plain handshake, with Mr. Harris, the buffer, between them. Dad and Mr. Kaufman grasped each other's hands too long because I think they didn't know what to say to each other. There was too much to say. It was like in a movie, where for a moment the world stops: freeze-frame, then fast-forward. I gazed up at the stars and thought of the fake ones spinning in Bobby's playroom. This was real.

As my father came toward me, Mrs. Kaufman stepped forward and brushed her hand on my arm as I passed by. "I'm so, so happy to see you, Daniel."

Relieved or happy? "Thank you." I forced a smile.

Then Bobby's mother took me by surprise. She gave me a hug—long enough to make me feel really uncomfortable. She looked down at me, teary-eyed, and glanced over at Dr. Kaufman, nodding, as if things were okay. Bobby waved to both of them.

Bobby had his father, who seemed like nothing ever bothered him; he had Max, running in circles, excited by all the kids milling around; and he had his mother. I got angry all over again at mine as I watched their family. Then it hit me as my father drove around the corner: maybe, just maybe, this was all an excuse, and my mother would have left anyway. Maybe it was just a matter of time and had nothing to do with the accident. Maybe it was good my mother wasn't here, because there would have been a scene at the party—that is, if she had come to the Kaufmans'. Or I wouldn't have been at Bobby's house at all because the scene would have started at ours weeks earlier.

Before we went inside Dad pulled me next to him on the small redwood deck outside our kitchen. We looked up at the clear night. "Boy, that's bright. Is that a planet or some sort of satellite?"

"It's the North Star—the one that guides you in the dark."

"So now you've got the answers. I remember when you were all questions."

"Like?" I asked.

"Like, where do people go when they die? Is there really a heaven? Or life on other planets?"

"Well, is there, Dad?"

"Could be—who knows? Maybe not life like we know it—like us. Maybe they're not as advanced." Dad gazed high above the big oak tree I used to climb.

"Maybe they're more intelligent. Are we so smart?"

My father squeezed my arm and stood closer.

"I'm sorry," I said.

"What are you sorry for?"

"For spoiling your vacation. For not wanting to see Mom. For all this." I looked down at my walker.

Dad grabbed me by both my arms and stared into my eyes. "Don't you ever apologize. Nothing was your fault. Things happen."

"Do you still blame the Kaufmans? And Mom for leaving?"

He got quiet, glanced upward, and sighed. "I don't know who or what to blame anymore."

"I wish this had never happened."

"Me too, Daniel." Then he looked down at me. "It's all been so frustrating. The whole thing. You know what I wish? For you to be in the May Meet. A positive goal. I'm done with blame, Daniel."

"Are you crazy? I haven't started swimming without a kickboard yet."

"By next year maybe you will."

"Next year?"

"New Year's Eve is in about a week. Ten days. That's next year. Have a little faith."

"Isn't that Mom's department?"

"Ah, a smidge can't hurt anyone. Believe in something."

"I believe in getting rid of this." I bopped the walker on its handlebar.

"Then you will. That's a fine thing to believe in."

So I made a wish on a star. Not one in particular. Any that might hear me.

Nineteen

Krista

There is no certainty; there is only adventure. Even stars explode.
—Roberto Assagioli, father of psychosynthesis

The first thing I did as part of my New Year's resolutions was to toss the Top Ten List. I didn't really help Daniel. I hurt him. I also didn't lose those five pounds. As a matter of fact, out of misery I gained a few more eating Entenmann's Walnut Danish Rings and Yodels. Glazed doughnut holes put me over the edge. I couldn't accept what is. Just because someone you're crazy about likes someone else, who happens to be your friend, doesn't make you stop liking him on the spot. Maybe *her,* but not him. You can't force feelings away. They seem to have a will of their own.

I was glad Lainie went to stay with her father at his parents' place out on Long Island over the Christmas vacation. She e-mailed us about a dozen times how much she missed Bobby and that he was the best kisser in the whole wide world. Gina zipped back to just Sandy and me, *How does she know that from her limited experience? Is there something she's not telling us?* After that, whenever Lainie's name came up on my screen, I hit delete. She sent so many messages, I felt as if she were cyberstalking me.

On New Year's Eve, I followed my mother into the kitchen. As she began to stir diced celery and carrots into hot soup and heat some biscuits, I asked, "Can Sandy sleep over? Her family was supposed to go away, but Eric didn't finish his college applications, so they had to cancel their trip. Lainie's gone. And Gina has a *nice* family who are celebrating tonight together." My mother gave me a look. "So, can I call her?" She gave me another look as if to say, *Of course you can.*

When Mom came downstairs after her shower, she had curls going every which way. Dad winked at her as he pulled up the collar on his tweed sports jacket. "Hey, wild woman."

She smiled at him, kissed both of us, and handed me a telephone number. "Where we can be reached. I'll keep my cell on." Then she projected in her best teacher voice, "We'll be home after midnight. So I'll say Happy New Year now. Let it be a good and healthy one."

Dad gave Matt an extra squeeze on his shoulder as they left, but Matt seemed to be in heaven, staring at the tadpole in prime position on our coffee table. Since all the other parents had said flat-out no, I got to take care of it. Or I should say Matt did.

Matt puckered his lips and stuffed a tissue up the sleeve of his bathrobe. "He's lonely."

I ruffled his hair and bent down to look into the tank. Matt put his head next to mine.

"Look, Krista, he's almost a frog."

"Yes, *she* is almost a full-fledged frog."

"My friend Zachary let his turtle go when it started smelling up his room."

"That's mean. It couldn't fend for itself."

"No, it wasn't. The turtle went to a pond at the Science Center, where he's with other turtles now. They take care of him. Zachary even got a letter inviting his family to a nature program over the vacation where his turtle's going to be a star."

"Well, good for Zachary's turtle. Our frog has no amphibian ambitions. It's content being a celebrity in our little classroom. Big fish in a small pond."

"Huh?" said Matt. "What fish?"

"Never mind." I rolled my eyes. "It's a good ending to your story."

Matt tapped the tank. "I hope your frog has a good ending too."

"Why wouldn't it? Of course it will," I said as I pulled out a stack of board games.

Sandy came over right before Matt started building hotels on the entire cheap side of the Monopoly board. "You're giving me a major migraine, you twerp. Stop arguing with me. I'm not selling you my single green property, which would give you another monopoly. Who do you think you are, the next Donald Trump?"

Sandy tried to ease the tension by changing the subject. "I like the French version we play in class with Madame Bertin. My favorite property is named after a pig—Place Pigalle." Matt started to laugh uncontrollably, holding his sides, making oinks and grunts.

"You're disgusting!" I shouted as he chased me around the coffee table with a soggy Kleenex that he took from his nose.

After a few rounds more, Matt the Mogul whined, "I'm bored."

We put a cartoon video on for him, which lulled him to sleep. Sandy helped me carry him like a sack of potatoes from the sofa to his bedroom. Then we dragged the small portable TV from the kitchen countertop into my room and sprawled out in the dark on my bed with the picture on, no sound, waiting for the ball to drop in Times Square.

Sandy curled up beside me and blew one of those lime-and-white-striped paper horns that unfurled like the tongue of a frog catching flies. When it snapped back, she said, "You never told me what you thought of Bobby's party."

I rolled over on my back, leaned into the pillow, pushed my hair up, and sighed.

"I know," she said softly.

"What do you know?"

"That you like him."

"Who?"

"You know who—Bobby."

I tightened inside.

"I've known you since you were four. You think you can hide things from me?"

"So why didn't you say anything?"

"Come on, Krista. Why didn't *you*? I thought we tell each other everything."

I didn't have an answer to that. It was just something I needed to keep to myself.

"Now I can tell you. Remember that valentine candy box from third grade?"

"The one that could feed a nation?"

"Well, yeah. I always thought Bobby gave it to me. It was Daniel."

"I thought so."

"Why?"

"I don't know, I just did. You two were so close." She twisted her ponytail around her index finger. "I've always liked Daniel."

"Me too."

She paused. "Like you like Bobby."

I turned on my side toward her. "You rat, you never told me."

"Like you never told me about Bobby. I didn't get a valentine in third grade from anyone but you and my stepbrother. When you got that box I was so jealous."

"You were?"

"Yes. *I am.*"

"Oh, Sandy. But I never knew it was from him."

"Would you have acted differently? Has Lainie?"

"But she doesn't know how I feel."

"Krista, *everyone* knows."

"Not Bobby!" I shrieked, freaking out.

She gulped. "Your eyes light up and you get so quiet when you see him."

I sighed. "It's weird the way sometimes you want something so much you can really kid yourself."

"Nah, we all dream," she said.

"What's yours?" I asked.

"To make the varsity soccer team next year."

"But you're amazing already," I protested on her behalf.

"No, I'm not. Not like Gina. And she hardly ever practices. All she does is work at her uncle's after school. Some people are lucky and born with talent. Like you've got for science. I think you're going to make a great doctor someday. You like helping people."

I put my head right next to Sandy's on the pillow and could feel her breath.

"So, what was it like to dance with Big Bad Bob?" she teased.

I elbowed her in the side.

"Ouch!" Sandy shouted, and I put my palm over her mouth so we wouldn't wake Matt.

"I felt as if I had bowling balls for feet. It was so . . ." I hesitated. "Not happening."

"And I guess you so wanted it to."

I nodded sadly. *Still do.* "What did you and Daniel talk about?"

I'm not sure why, but I hoped it wasn't about the stars. His stars.

"Remember how Daniel got everyone to do the bunny hop during gym at the fifth-grade Heart Association Jumpathon before his accident? And Coach was at the head of the conga line, his love handles jiggling with each hop back and then forward, forward, forward?"

"Yeah?" I wondered where this was going.

"Well, Daniel asked me to dance. His way, right now. And he got Gina to join in, even though she was upset, and then Harry. Daniel knows how to make lemonade out of lemons."

"So do you, Sandy, my glass-half-full pal."

She smiled deeply. Sandy would be good with Daniel. But my heart felt pierced. Daniel and I had been through so much together—why hadn't he felt comfortable enough to ask me to dance? At least he hadn't shown her Orion's belt.

Gina rang up a minute before twelve. We screamed together, "Happy New Year!" as I jumped up and down with Sandy and we watched colored confetti drop down on thousands in the crowd in Times Square.

My parents called anyway, saying, "We wish you the world."

Minutes after midnight, I decided to start the year right. I got the valentine box from my closet and threw it in the wastebasket under my desk. The crumpled note slipped onto my rug. Sandy picked it up. She crinkled her eyebrows as she silently read it: *Krista Harris do you love me?*

"This is *not* Daniel's handwriting."

"What?" I took the note from her and examined it.

"It's Bobby's! See the funny dot thing? He always does that above his *i*'s and makes that tail on the *a*'s."

"This is going to make me nuts."

Let it go. Let it go.

So much for fresh new starts.

Twenty

Daniel

*If ever there was a time to take a chance on yourself,
the time is now.*
—Senator Charles Schumer

Monday morning our group met. It was my turn to report on the tadpole, but Krista had taken it over the vacation and we hadn't talked since Bobby's party. I peered
into the tank without looking at her as she placed it on
the wide bookshelf. "So, little guy, how ya doing? In a few
weeks your lungs will be developed and you'll beat me in
our race."

Lainie heard me as she dumped leftover candy canes
on each of our desks. "Just because you don't have
webbed feet doesn't mean you can't win."

"Guess I'll wear flippers," I responded as I watched
Krista sift through her notes.

"Some frogs hibernate underground at the bottom of
a pond, burrowing beneath debris, while the African
water frog takes about three months to evolve from a tadpole to a frog," Krista announced.

"Lying low for the winter." Brandon did his usual eyebrow wiggle.

"Our tadpole could go into a freshwater pond when the weather's warm," Krista said. She straightened her back and looked up from her page at the rest of the group.

"Release him?" I searched her eyes for some sanity. "Into the wild?"

Krista stared at Lainie's loafer, butted up against the side of Bobby's sneaker. Lainie gave him a playful nudge with her foot and left it against his. A few moments later Krista turned to me. "Uh-huh, let him go."

Bobby cleared his throat. "That's not your decision to make. The class is a team."

"Right," Lainie agreed. "And Mr. James would be real ticked off."

"What about taking care of itself? And food?" I pressed on, totally amazed at her.

"At first I thought that too. My little brother is actually the one who put the idea in my head to set it free. His friend donated his pet turtle to the Science Center, so it's not really fending for itself. In the end I figure the turtle's probably doing a lot better there than in his friend's bedroom. And we can give the center our data on the frog's growth." She looked around the room at us. "You're all acting like I'm tossing it down the toilet bowl."

Bobby paused. "Releasing it into the wild? I don't know." He shook his head.

"Maybe it will be a pig in mud, swimming around in a bigger pond instead of a crummy little plastic tank, going nowhere," Krista wondered out loud.

I looked into her big green eyes. "A *frog* in mud."

"Yeah, a frog in mud," she repeated as the bell rang.

"To be continued," Bobby stated.

And Krista said with a tone, "Why do you always get the last word?"

Everyone got real quiet. I think we were all shocked. That was more Gina than Krista.

The trial judge in my dad's hearing recessed early, so my father picked me up after school. We bumped into Lainie and her mother, who seemed to be preoccupied with makeup at the checkout counter in Beacon Pharmacy. Lainie turned red and covered a box of Tampax with her hand when she saw me. I was reminded of spring, fifth grade. The girls left with Miss Healy to have their health talk while the boys remained with Coach. When Coach brought up the topic of nocturnal emissions, Brandon, whose father was a car mechanic, asked, "Why are we talking about auto inspections? Aren't they done only during the daytime?"

There was snickering in the back and Coach responded, "No—like in wet dreams."

Jeremy waved his hand to get Coach's attention. "I dreamed of the beach."

Harry came up with the clever observation that "dreams

are neither wet or dry." When everyone began to crack up, he gazed around, like, *What's with you guys?*

It became immediately clear that there was more to this discussion than levels of humidity or the time of day. Coach sighed, glaring at bleachers lined with, at the time, mostly eleven-year-old boys. "I think I've got my work cut out for me."

A light went on in Brandon's head after Harry, who had an older brother in tenth grade, whispered in his ear, explaining the gritty details. "Oh!" he cried, realizing what Coach meant—like in dreaming about sex— and naturally Brandon raised his hand again. "You mean like when my cousin told me he thinks about getting all hot and bothered, and it's like a leaky faucet down there." Well, all bedlam broke loose.

When the hubbub quieted down, Coach said, "Thanks for sharing that plumbing analogy."

The rest of us wished we had ended up like the girls, with a pink booklet full of diagrams and lots of line drawings and a title like "Growing Up: Your Body and You." I think that afternoon took its toll on Coach, because even though he looks like a big bruiser, at the end of the session he seemed totally wasted. There were rumors that more detailed information in the curriculum was scheduled for when we were in middle school. And I personally was waiting. Now that I actually am in middle school, I still am eager and waiting.

All this went through my head as I stood in the

drugstore. I gave Lainie an understanding smile, and she tried to smile back. "See ya," I said after my father paid for a new set of earplugs at the cash register, nodding pleasantly at Lainie and her mother.

"See ya." She bounded out of the store after her mother, who didn't give me the how-are-you-doing? smile. Nothing. And it was our first face-to-face since the accident. Of course, my father and Mrs. Michaels had about as much in common as Oscar and Felix.

After the pharmacy, my father and I went to the Y to practice my lame attempt at dolphin kicks, which were more guppy than dolphin. When we came out to the pool, a string of red, white, and blue triangular flags dangled several feet above the water. Two rows of bleachers were set up along the side. A lifeguard was closing off lanes so the public couldn't swim.

"What's up?" my father asked the lifeguard.

"A sign-up for age groups swimming for all the area schools, and then a practice session for the May Meet."

I stood there with my beach towel draped over my walker. "Did you know?" I asked my father.

He seemed distracted. "No."

"Really?" I pressed, while Bobby, several teammates, and Coach walked in.

My dad looked bothered, watching the swimmers my age signing up. "Really."

Is he telling the truth? I wondered.

I wanted to leave. I wanted to stay. Both feelings swelled up in me at the same time. We stayed. We sat on the bleachers with that old urge to see who the competition was, and watch others swim like I used to swim. Like people always say when they haven't tried something for a long time, "It's like riding a bike. You never forget." My mind didn't. My body did.

Coach came over and sat down next to us. "Come to sign up?"

I wanted to say, *Are you smoking something?* Instead, I said, "Yeah, right."

"Why not? You're getting stronger each day. I've seen you do a few steps without this." He put his hand on my walker. "The meet is months away. It's a goal."

I noticed Bobby doing sit-ups on an exercise mat. "An unrealistic one."

"Daniel, you were my top swimmer. The strongest. Don't cripple your spirit."

Nice word, Coach. Real sensitive. "*I* didn't cripple anything."

He gave me a rabbit punch in the arm and pushed a clipboard in my face.

I pushed the list of names away. Bobby's name was at the top. My dad sighed. He and Coach just looked at each other, and Coach put his arm around my father. He then patted me on the back and walked away, yelling at everyone, "Stretch before doing freestyle to avoid cramps!" He looked over at me and gave me a thumbs-up to show he was okay with whatever I decided, even if my father wasn't. I gave him a thumbs-up back.

The first heat was of eight people in each of the eight

lanes. One way was the breaststroke, and the return was the backstroke. Bobby burst out full speed ahead. The parents who had stayed were shouting, "Come on" from the sidelines, and this wasn't even the real thing! With each person diving into a lane, I'd think, *Move that way, breathe on that moment, accelerate to the wall, turn around faster.* It stressed me out watching the sprint. My brain was doing the motions. It was like when my mother watched another violinist, giving her interpretation movement by movement. She'd criticize the way the bow was held, the position of the pinky, the fingering of a cadenza, the vibratos, the musician's intonation. "Each artist has their own way, like each swimmer," she confided in me.

My mother was giving up classical violin for now, playing without a net because she was taking a chance on something new. Wasn't that scary? Mom had once said, "I need music like breathing air." I knew what air I needed. I rolled the walker over and put my name on the clipboard for the May Meet.

Coach clapped his hands together. "Lookin' good, Rosen." I smiled at him.

When I got back to my seat, I told my father, "I don't want the aide in my classroom anymore."

"Isn't it up to the school? A mandate?" Dad asked. "You'll be okay on your own?"

"I'm not on my own, I have friends. I get around most of the time without her. Is she with me in the locker room? Or the lunchroom? Or at home? So wait, I *am* on my own, aren't I?"

My father half smiled.

"This is the way it has to be," I told him.

"Guess I can't buckle you up and put you in a car seat anymore. Those days are over."

I half smiled back at him.

Bobby came over to the bleachers, dripping wet after the relays were over. "A bunch of us are going to the movies afterward. It starts in about forty-five minutes. Wanna come? We're all meeting there."

I looked over at my father but didn't wait for his answer. "Sure." As Bobby walked away, I got up. "You'd like to sit in the back of the theater and wait in case anything happens, right, Dad? Well, the biggest thing might be a soda spill. Wait, I thought of something worse. My walker might get stuck on a wad of gum," I said sarcastically.

"All parents wish they could always protect their child," Dad said gently.

"You can't. Guess we both learned that."

A while later, Dad drove me to the multiplex near Main Street. He let out a deep sigh. "Ah, the old RKO. Boarded up. There was a gilded fountain in the gold lobby. Moroccan fretwork. An azure sky above the balcony. Not just any blue—the most magical blue you ever saw. It almost made you want to fly. And there were matrons in crisp white uniforms shushing us on Saturday afternoons, rotating flashlights in our direction as we shared a bucket of popcorn back and forth and rattled boxes of stale malt balls."

"Sounds like fun." I smirked.

"Actually, it was. Total escapism. As your mother might say, I became one with the screen." Dad paused, probably stuck on thinking about Mom. "Years later, when your mother and I dated, we watched double features on a loveseat upstairs. We'd smuggle in a meatball hero for dinner. The whole evening cost me under ten dollars. Sometimes I was a big spender and treated your mother to hot coffee and an extra-large chocolate-chip cookie. She loved those big bakery cookies."

"She still does."

"I know." Dad smiled. "So the deal is, I'm walking you in. For me, not you."

We waited by the candy counter. No one showed up. Finally I said, "Let's go."

Dad pulled me back by my ski jacket. "Maybe they're already sitting down." We went into the darkened theater, and I followed him up the center aisle, holding on to him. He narrowed his eyes. "Aren't those boys from your class?" I hate it when parents show you that you're wrong and they're right.

I squinted, my eyes gradually adjusting to the dark. My father led me and we stopped by a leg stretched way out—Bobby's. He moved over when he saw me and put his jacket on the seat in front of him, leaving me the aisle seat. "How's it going?"

"It's going." I nodded.

"See you when it's over," Dad whispered in my ear. "Out front. If you need me, call my cell. I'll be in the library doing some research on the microfiche."

"Okay." I wanted to get rid of him.

"Are these seats taken?" Lainie pushed past me.

"Thought it was going to be just us guys," Brandon said to Bobby, adding loudly, "The chick flick is in theater two. This is an *action* movie."

"I like action," Gina fired back. She balanced a giant soda and box of Raisinets as she sat in the seat right behind him instead of next to Lainie.

"Oh, yeah?" Brandon turned around to face her.

"If I wanted a lot of scenery, I'd go to the park." Gina flicked a chocolate-covered raisin at him.

I chuckled. Sandy edged past our knees to sit next to Gina. Krista was next, her sneakers clinging to the sticky floor. When she saw Bobby, a crease furrowed her forehead and she plopped down next to Gina instead of in our row. Lainie eased between Bobby and Brandon on Bobby's other side. After the main feature started, and the music began, Bobby draped his arm on the back of Lainie's seat. The rest of us ripped strings of red licorice, thin and long as shoelaces, into bits, sitting at the edge of our seats during the car crashes and explosions. When a caramelized nut dropped into Lainie's lap from the Cracker Jack box, Bobby scooped it up into his mouth and she giggled. He rubbed Lainie's knee so effortlessly, as if it were nothing and he did it every day. When Gina jammed the back of Brandon's seat with her foot, his M&M's fell off the armrest, and he scrambled around on the floor searching for his missing candy, making everyone hiss together, "Quiet!" What was he going to do if he found them? Eat them?

During the credits, Bobby turned to me. "Did you like the movie?"

"Pretty dumb," I overheard Gina say to Krista. "They should return our money."

"It was okay," I answered Bobby as we all filed up the aisle.

"Want to practice together? I see you signed up for the May Meet over the Memorial Day weekend."

Krista gave me a look of surprise as I nodded to Bobby.

On the way into the lobby, Krista stuffed her hands in her coat pockets. "That's great, Daniel. You finally decided to really go for it again."

"It's the easiest event, Krista. Nothing fancy. Freestyle swimming. Not the butterfly. I'm not nuts."

She kicked a gummy worm out of our path. "I'll still help you if you want."

I tossed an empty candy box in the garbage as we were leaving the theater, and took in a breath. "If you want to."

"I do."

And I smiled. Not a half smile. One wide and full.

Twenty-One

Krista

Being yourself is going to be the hardest thing you do in your life.
—Whoopi Goldberg, comedian

It seemed New York City had more snow than Alaska that January. My mother put her hands on her hips and declared, "If I have one more snow day with you and Matt going at each other, I won't be held responsible." Whatever the unspecified crime was, it didn't prevent Matt from begging her to take us ice-skating. "Only if you wear two layers of long underwear," she insisted, stuffing him in a snowsuit until he could barely move, let alone skate. He looked like a little Buddha.

When she was done, she gave him a big hug, and he cuddled into her. "I love you!" said Matt.

"I love you too," my mother said.

"But who do you love more?" I egged her on. "*Me* or Matt?"

"Here we go again." She rolled her eyes, something I usually did. "I love you equally."

"You're supposed to say that, but I know the truth," I said as Mom wiped the tip of Matt's nose.

Matt pushed the tissue away with his mitten and grinned. "She loves *me* more."

"The truth is, when Matt drives me crazy, I love you more, and when you drive me crazy, I love him more. Right now, you're both treading on thin ice. No pun intended."

"Real funny," I said.

We followed her on the pine-needle path into Bowne Park. When we got to the frozen pond in the center, the sign read SKATING TODAY.

Clouds drifted in a colorless sky as we skated in a row, holding Matt up between us as he wobbled on his ankles. After a while, we took a break and sat on a bench in the crisp winter air. Mom unscrewed a thermos she had brought from home. Cinnamon-scented vapors spiraled up my nostrils. She poured three cups of mulled cider and handed me one. "Your father and I love you and your brother to infinity. *More* than infinity."

On the way back, we stopped off for Chinese takeout. I couldn't wait to open my fortune cookie and see what words of wisdom were printed on the white strip of paper inside. *Treasure what you have.* I tucked the saying in my pocket to throw in my drawer alongside the love note. I had kept it, even though I no longer had the candy box to fill with treasures. I still felt confused about the penmanship mystery—how Bobby's script had ended up on a note inside a valentine box that Daniel had given me. And why?

Later that afternoon, on my way home, before the sun sank, I noticed Bobby's dirt bike outside Lainie's house, leaning against the garbage cans on her driveway. Seeing his bike was a reminder that something was over. Not between me and Bobby—that never was—but between me and me. Something inside me knew that this spring I could no longer ride over to Twenty-seventh Avenue wishing he would notice me. Something was gone, and it was never going to feel the same. It had changed the night of Bobby's party. Never again would there be silly notes with little boxes for yes, I love you, and no, I don't, or parties *without* kissing. Even projects like growing frogs would seem babyish. Next year in science, we'd probably be *dissecting* frogs or pigs' hearts and other gross things like that, which I was looking forward to. Everything was changing. It was scary and exciting and disappointing, like the time I was slow-dancing with Bobby and didn't know what to expect.

Nighttime came early. When I glanced out the window while I was petting my cat, Rosie, I noticed Bobby's bike was still out front. The streetlight shined on Lainie walking him over to it. Neither of them saw me spying from behind the drapes of my living room window. They kissed on the lips. I wanted to turn away, but at the same time I was drawn to watching, like some people do when they pass a car accident on the highway and can't turn away. She put her hand on the back of his neck and smoothed his hair, kissing him on the cheek. Then they waved good-bye. As he rode away, she toppled on the ice while carrying a garbage can to the strip of driveway between the two split-level houses. Like roadkill, she remained sprawled out. Without thinking, I ran outside and across the street to help her up. Tears clung to her lashes as she brushed away the dirty snow.

She looked up, surprised to see me. "What are you doing here?"

"I was scratching Rosie at the window when you fell."

"You're going to get sick out here without a jacket. Come on in."

I hesitated.

She looked at me pleadingly.

"Sure," I agreed.

"My mother's going to lose it when she sees my new jeans." She tried to hide the hole, but the denim patch continued to flap in the wind, exposing a raw, bloody knee.

I put my arm under hers. "She'll survive."

"She works hard to support us."

"So do you."

She leaned on me as we went inside her kitchen.

Lainie poured milk into two tall cobalt-blue glasses, pushing away the package of low-fat wafers on the counter. She took two blondies from the freezer and nuked them. While we waited, I washed her knee at the kitchen sink. She winced when the washcloth touched her wound. When the microwave stopped beeping, I took out the paper plate and she sat down on the chair next to me, pushing the larger blondie toward me.

"I shouldn't. I gained winter weight over the holidays," I admitted.

"You? You look fine," she said.

"You're being nice. If it were you, you'd shoot yourself."

"No," she said, "my mother would do it for me. We could share one blondie." She cut the bigger one in half and gave me a piece. "Listen, I need to talk."

"What's up?" I asked, wondering if it was about Bobby.

She poked at the milk carton before answering. "I feel funny."

"About what?"

"About telling anyone."

I leaned closer and put my hand over hers. "What? You can tell me."

She took a deep breath. "You know how I'm a klutz and I trip a lot?"

I didn't want to nod and say, *Yeah, you make Chevy Chase and his falling act on the old* SNL *look like nothing*, because I didn't want to make her feel bad. But I sometimes wondered, like Gina, whether Lanie did it to get attention.

Thank God she went on without looking up at me, staring at my hand instead. "Before I lived here, I used to wear these clunky brown leather corrective shoes that went way up my ankles. Trust me, they didn't look like those hip boots." She slid a thick silver ring nervously up and down her middle finger. "For four years, I slept at night on my back with an iron brace between my legs to straighten out my feet. You know how they say when a limb is amputated the person often senses that part of their body even though it's gone—phantom pain? Well, I still feel that brace even though it's off. I feel it in my mind."

"Oh, Lain." I squeezed her hand gently.

"I never wore party shoes. You know the kind—the patent leather ones with the delicate strap near the ankle and bow near the toes. The other kids made fun of me at birthday parties if I was invited." She lowered her voice to a whisper. "One girl used to call me 'Clubfoot.' I felt so ashamed to be singled out like that. When I came here in second grade and no longer needed the brace or the shoes, I wore my first really nice pair to your birthday party when you turned eight. It was great not standing out. Well, Gina made a comment on why I was so dressed up and girly." We both smiled at the thought of Gina, always barefoot or in sneakers. "Everyone wants to fit in. Or prove something. Except you."

"Me?" I said, thinking of how I wanted to fit in with Bobby instead of Daniel.

"Yeah, you. You seem to go your own way."

"I do?" My voice went up.

"Gina's so in-your-face. Sandy wants to make nice. You're original."

Lainie made me wonder, because that's what Gina had said about Lainie. "No two people are alike. Isn't everyone an original? You think you model because you want to fit in? You need to shine. I'm not saying that in a bad way. It's who you are."

She smiled and put her other hand on top of mine.

"I'm sure Sandy will be happy to lend you the red patent leather shoes that she wore to Bobby's party," I teased.

"I will never speak to you again if you tell anyone. Cross your heart, Krista Harris."

I made an X over my heart.

"And if there is ever a movie version of my life you will be written out of it permanently or at the very least scandalized in the tabloids if you leak my secret."

"I promise."

She limped to the washer and dryer and grabbed a bunny slipper from the laundry basket. "Here, take it. Then give me the left one from your pair of dog slippers. That way we'll always be able to think of each other as sisters."

I smiled and took it, then let out a sigh. "I have something to tell you too."

Lainie moved her chair closer even though we were alone. Could I trust her?

"Now it's my turn to share a secret. I've liked . . ." I stopped.

"What?" She made a cross over her heart too.

"I've liked Bobby for a long time."

"Who doesn't?" she said, apparently not realizing what I meant. "He likes you too."

"I mean *like* like. How he likes you. I can't believe I'm telling you this, but I thought he gave me a love note in third grade."

"Oh," she said casually. "Ms. Sanchez's class was busier than a post office that year."

I let out a little laugh. She looked into my eyes, and this time she realized. "I'm sorry, Krista. I didn't know."

"No one knew. I thought. Anyway, I see now that Bobby never really liked me. Not in *that* way."

"You mean like how Daniel likes you?"

"What do you mean?" I asked her. My throat was dry. I didn't want to tell her that the valentine candy was from Daniel. It was between us, like the swimming.

"For a smart person, Krista, you're pretty dumb."

I looked at her. I was. I am.

"Daniel has always looked at you like you're the most perfect person on the planet."

"He has?" *Not the night of the party,* I thought.

"And why not? You're kind, Krista. To everyone. Look at you. How nice you are to Daniel. Now look at me. Here I had this big thing with my legs in a brace as a kid, and now Daniel has stuff with his, and have I been there for him? No," she whispered. "I haven't, really."

"I don't feel that kind."

Lainie leaned over to hug me and I hugged her back. I thought of all the things I said to myself about Daniel and Bobby—and her, even now. I couldn't stop thinking that Lainie would always remember her first kiss was with Bobby and I would always remember that mine wasn't. Still, somehow I knew our secrets would remain something we shared in a moment of strength and not weakness. What surprised me most was that Lainie and I shared any secrets at all.

We went into her roped-off living room and played a duet together on the piano of "Heart and Soul."

As we sat in near darkness, Lainie's mother walked in, flipped on the light switch, and tossed a black leather portfolio down on a side table. Lainie looked caught, although she hadn't done anything wrong.

Mrs. Michaels said through gritted teeth, "Something on your shoulder appeared in a final mock-up of a print ad. A tattoo. The client said that was not how he wanted his product portrayed. I spent my afternoon convincing him and the modeling agency to airbrush it out. Do you know how that star suddenly appeared?"

Lainie looked down, covering the scrape on her knee with her hand. Her mom didn't notice.

"And what jerk gave an underage kid a tattoo? I want the name and address. I'm reporting them." She put out her raised palm as if Lainie were going to hand over a receipt.

"I don't know," said Lainie with a shrug. "I paid in cash."

I still admired Lainie for following through on something that was important to her that day, even though it was for something I would never ever do. "I was with her," I said, trying to defend Lainie. "She gave it a lot of thought."

Lainie looked at me, her lower lip trembling. "It was my decision. Mine alone."

Her mother said to me, "You know better. Your father's in the health industry. You see what can happen to people. Look at that boy Daniel." She turned to Lainie and her eyes filled with tears. "A beautiful young girl like you. To scar and ruin yourself like that. You're having it removed with a laser. I already called a doctor."

"No, I'm not!" Lainie's voice cracked.

Her mother exploded, "If your father were around, this wouldn't have happened."

What did *that* have to do with anything? Mrs. Michaels had enough discipline for two.

I backed away toward the door. "I have to go home and help make dinner."

Lainie looked as if I was deserting her.

As I closed the door I heard Lainie weeping and her mom's raised voice. "Guess you spoiled your appetite for dinner. Blondies?"

Guiltily, I whacked a long twig against Lainie's bedroom window after dinner. She let me in the side door, and I handed her a shopping bag with my single dog slipper, with its slightly chipped brown glass eye. She put on the mismatched set—the long ears of a bunny and a dog dragging on the floor. As I followed her into the hall, her hand went to her chest. "I can't breathe. My mother has to be in every part of my life. When is she going to realize that I'm a separate person from her?" She stroked her eyebrow as if she had a migraine headache. "My tattoo is staying."

"I know it is." I placed my hand on her shoulder over the spot where the tattoo remained.

"Can I come home with you, Krista? I don't want to stay here."

"Oh, Lain," was all I could say, knowing my parents wouldn't allow it.

Her mother was in the living room, sitting in front of the TV in an old terry-cloth robe. She looked disheveled, her hair uncombed. Had I ever seen her without makeup? Somehow she looked younger, even though she stared at me through dark-ringed, shadowed, vacant eyes, sipping a diet soda from a can. Lainie brushed past her.

"Sorry." I smiled awkwardly. Then I followed Lainie to her room.

Her floor was a mess, clothes strewn everywhere. Her desk was open, the drawers in shambles like a burglar had been searching through pieces of her life. Family snapshots from when she was little were spread across her bed: Lainie perched on her father's shoulders at the beach, waves crashing; reading with her mother on the front porch; the three of them together on an amusement park ride. There were also professional photos of Lainie in bikinis, nightgowns, evening dresses—looking thirty instead of turning thirteen at the end of this summer.

We both glanced up when we noticed her mother in the hall. I hadn't heard her footsteps, but now I realized her breathing was heavy and uneven. Lainie ignored her as she continued to sort through her things. Her overnight bag was out and packed.

Her mother came into the bedroom, eyes bulging like a bulldog's. Lainie coolly went over to the open drawer, grabbed a pair of scissors from next to her plastic Peanuts pencil case, and held the sharp points in the air. "Stay away from me!" she ordered, and she began to cut the portfolio photos in pieces.

Shaking, her mother strode over and repeated, "Stay away from you?" She slapped Lainie across the face.

I stood there frozen. Lainie's cheek was red when her mother took her hand away. She was still holding the scissors in the air. Without shedding a single tear, she took an African violet from her night table with her free hand and dumped it on the plush cream-colored carpet at her mother's feet, the dirt spreading like flakes of pepper on an omelet.

I carefully took the scissors out of Lainie's hand—her palm was sweaty like mine, and she squeezed my hand. As I left with the scissors, Lainie began to crumple all the pretty pictures, all the years of her life, and I prayed that I wouldn't hear about her and her mother on the eleven o'clock news.

Twenty-Two

Daniel

It is good to have an end to journey toward;
but it is the journey that matters, in the end.
—*Ursula K. Le Guin, author*

On a cold, gray morning with dead maple leaves caught in tree roots and vines, I took Bobby up on his offer to do some laps. His father drove. Their SUV was so high off the ground I could have used a ladder as I climbed in the back, knees first, on the floor. Dr. Kaufman turned around and rushed out of the car to help me, but I lifted myself up with all the strength I had. He gave me a look of surprise when I eased into the seat. "How's it going?"

"It's going," I answered him.

"And your dad?" he asked, sliding behind the steering wheel again.

"Working," I lied, knowing he had avoided coming outside to say hello.

It was so uncomfortably quiet in the car the rest of the way that I wondered, *Was this a good idea?*

I swam for the first time without a kickboard as Bobby's father clocked him. I used to hate feeling his dad's eyes on me, watching my moves, but now it felt awful that I was no longer considered the competition. The longer we swam, the faster Bobby seemed to go and the slower I went. Why had I signed up for the meet? Temporary insanity?

"You're doing great!" Bobby shouted to me from his lane.

"Yeah, right!" I shouted back. "For the toddler class," which was amusingly named the Tadpoles.

He ducked under the ropes into my lane. I looked over at his father, who began to pace as Bobby broke the flow of his laps. "Sorry, I know this was supposed to be our practice. I didn't know he would stay. Next time, we'll do it alone. He's acting like this is a four-hundred-meter medley."

I held on to the wall and caught my breath. "No sweat. I understand. Parents."

"We just got this amazing heater for the pool in our backyard so I can have unlimited time, extending the seasons. They're getting it ready the end of March. So you'll come?"

I thought of practicing with Bobby. With Krista.

Dr. Kaufman cupped his hands, shouting, "Are you guys cooling down already?"

"Dad, I'm not going for the gold here!" Bobby blurted out.

So he sat on a deck chair and left us alone at our own pace the rest of the session.

I wasn't sure what made me more wasted: the practice or Bobby's father.

"How'd it go?" my father asked, looking up from a brief when I walked in the door.

"Intense."

"Bob Kaufman?"

"Well, you know him. He was okay."

"Yeah. Bobby's dad loves him and figures Bobby better do it now or never. I think your mother had some dreams of her own for you."

"I guess I disappointed her." I had, hadn't I?

"Not ever."

"Coach told us our edge is to have heart. And passion. It's the doing more than the winning. He said, 'It's the journey' and 'Push yourselves to the end. To the very last second, because if you give up a second too soon, you can lose.' Mom's giving up a second too soon."

My father's eyes clouded. "That doesn't mean *you* have to lose."

I hesitated for a moment.

"Dad?"

"Yes?" he answered.

"Are you and Mom getting separated?"

"Well, we aren't living together right now," he said.

"You know, divorced."

He sighed. "That's not what this is about. At least not from my end."

"Then what is it? She can't act like she's just visiting her sister anymore."

"No, she can't."

"Then what's wrong?"

"I don't know *exactly* what is wrong. Maybe even she doesn't really know, at least not completely. She's going to have to let us know when she's ready. On her own time. I do know that she'd better be honest with you when that time comes. And it better come," he said with conviction.

"Do you still love her?" I asked.

"I've been with your mother for over twenty years. I love her. I just don't *like* her right now." He shuffled his hands in his lap.

"You're a very patient person, Dad."

He gave a deep laugh. "If you had heard us on the phone the other night going at it, I doubt you'd be saying that."

I lowered my voice. "She's coming home, right?"

"I can't promise anything, but I can hope."

Dad wasn't giving up a second too soon. He had heart. And he had passion.

I went into Mom's studio and found a passage in the *Tao Te Ching* by the sixth-century Chinese philosopher Lao-tzu. It was marked with a red silk ribbon bookmark, the page still opened, as if she had just left the room to spread peanut butter on whole wheat bread with blobs of grape jelly for lunch and was coming right back.

> *We shape clay into a pot,*
> *but it is the emptiness inside*
> *that holds whatever you want.*

I guess I wasn't as enlightened as my mother. Maybe it would take a few more lives and centuries to understand.

Twenty-Three

Krista

The strings of my heart have snapped.
—Book of Job

Lainie and her mother did not appear in any news head-lines. Her mom even drove her to school three days in a row, so Lainie wouldn't be late for homeroom when she overslept. The fourth day, she entered right as the bell rang and Mr. James was writing on the board: *Frog time!* He faced the class, waving two fingers in the air in a "V" sign to get our full attention. "Quiet down, guys. Our tad-pole has grown up. In celebration of all your care, we're going on a class trip in a few weeks."

Everyone grinned as he passed out permission slips. Brandon raised his hand and spoke out before Mr. James had a chance to call on him. "I have nothing against the Museum of Natural History or the planetarium, but we've gone every year since kindergarten. If I see one more galaxy or dinosaur or gem exhibit, I'm going to barf."

Mr. James put his hand up for Brandon to stop, then

grinned impishly in Bobby's direction. Bobby smiled as if he'd won the lottery, which made Brandon pause. "Bobby's grandfather has generously offered to show us how to make candy at his shop."

Brandon looked as if he'd gone to heaven. Chocolate heaven.

He poked Bobby. "How come you didn't tell me?"

"Mr. James pledged me to secrecy."

"You'd be good in the CIA."

"But not under tickle torture," admitted Bobby.

"I'll have to remember that," Lainie said, smiling mischievously as she did a ten-digit wiggle toward Bobby's armpits.

On the day of the trip, Valentine's Day, everyone showed up with aprons for the scene of the crime: Kaufman's Chocolates.

"Borrow one from Omar the tent maker?" Brandon asked Sandy as we loaded onto the bus.

Sandy's cheeks turned pink. "My stepbrother bakes bread. It's *his* apron."

She looked over at Daniel lifting one that was sizes too big. "My father's," he said.

Sandy rested her hand on Daniel's walker so it wouldn't roll down the aisle to the front. It was nice seeing him on the bus with us without the aide by his side.

The noise level rose when the driver pulled in front of a shop with striped awnings and A. KAUFMAN, CHOCOLATIER etched on the window. Among pink stuffed animals holding white wicker baskets overflowing with candies were fancy heart-shaped boxes displayed in different sizes. The largest one was exactly the same kind I had gotten from Daniel.

"Single file," Mr. James ordered as we headed toward the back of the store, past glass cases filled with doily-lined plates of homemade fudge, nougats, and jellied fruits. Jade-green tiled walls hadn't changed since Bobby's great-grandfather had bought the store in the 1940s. An overpowering chocolate smell was rich in the air. Antique cast-iron molds decorated a display behind the cash register. Bins of cocoa, jars of cherries as red as a clown's nose, and assorted nuts were stacked on shelves. Mr. James shook the hand of the short, white-haired man welcoming us. "I suspect many of you already know Mr. Kaufman, who owns this store. I bet a lot of allowance money has been spent here."

"And deposited in our stomachs," Brandon added, checking out the fudge.

Mr. Kaufman stroked his thick, snowy mustache. "Many of you teethed on my treats."

"Which caused our first cavities," Brandon joked comfortably with him.

Standing next to his grandson, Abe was the same height as Bobby. Their eyes twinkled the same sea blue. Abe reminded me of my grandpa who had died—thick Russian accent, clear eyes the size of marbles, a voice that sounded like a frog's when he croaked, "Hello, darlink."

"There are a few rules you must follow in my kitchen

today," said his grandfather as he tied a stained cloth apron around his thick waist.

"Here it comes." Brandon folded his arms across his chest. "Rules."

"First, call me Abe. Rule number one: lick your fingers while dipping."

Everyone giggled.

"Rule number two: never lick your neighbor's fingers."

The laughter got louder.

"And rule number three: your eyes should be bigger than your stomach. Feel free to nosh while you work. Everyone get that?"

We all nodded. Brandon said, "I'm tasting *everything*."

"Good. Then I'll show you different kinds of chocolate and how to coat fruit."

"Mr. K," Brandon yelled out. "Fruit? Like in nutritious?"

Mr. Kaufman nodded.

"Well, almost everything," Brandon amended. Gina picked up a dried fig and popped it in her mouth with attitude.

Bobby's grandfather held a fresh strawberry over a huge pot of melted chocolate. "It's important to know how to swirl. It's all in the wrist."

We imitated his motion in the air. I swirled a plump dried apricot into a bowl filled to the rim with warm bittersweet chocolate. Then we dipped Abe's square mocha marshmallows.

Lainie pushed the candy aside. "I'm sticking with fresh fruit."

"Come on." Gina pushed her marshmallow over on the wax-paper-covered cookie sheet.

I looked at Lainie, remembering what she'd said when we were alone. "Let her do what she wants."

Gina and Sandy exchanged looks.

Next, up and down the long worktable, we poured, splattered, and smoothed different kinds of chocolate into plastic heart-shaped lollipop molds. After they cooled and hardened, Abe handed each of us a small red box and a few silver foil ruffled paper liners. "Fill these with the candy you made. And here's a bag for the lollipops."

"Save them until you get home!" Mr. James piped in. "That's all I need—twenty-five kids bouncing off the walls in a massive sugar attack."

Then Abe took us to a clean workspace near his corner office. "This is where I print up on the computer, with the help of my techie grandson, the name of each chocolate and where it is in the box. I got that idea from that young man over there, when he was just a pip-squeak." He pointed to Daniel. "He told me, 'Put a plan, like a map of the constellations, in your double-decker assortment.' And I took this little *mirashker's* advice."

Daniel smiled proudly.

"I insert a map under the lid, then shrink-wrap the box, put a pretty ribbon on top, and presto, I'm in business!" *So that's how the note was done. Slipped in by them. That was their plan. But which one wrote it?*

Daniel nervously fingered the red ribbon around his

cellophane bag of lollipops as he saw me eyeing a heart-shaped box of chocolates in the basket of his walker. "Abe gave it to me. For old times' sake. They're his Mocha Mallows. He knows they're my favorite from when Bobby and I used to ride our bikes over."

"The mocha marshmallows are my favorite too."

He extended his hand and gave me the box.

"It's yours." I pushed it back. "I couldn't."

"Take it," he insisted.

"Daniel." I looked into his eyes.

"No strings attached. Happy Valentine's Day, Krista."

"You too, Daniel," I said softly. "Thanks."

The following day, my heart was pounding the whole bus ride to school in anticipation of what I was about to do. When I got into homeroom and thought no one was looking, I slipped the love note out of my backpack and onto Bobby's desk. Bobby was writing down his last observations about the frog on the chart when Brandon turned around as if he had radar. "Hey, Kaufman, Harris left something for you under your loose-leaf."

My cheeks were burning. Bobby walked slowly past me over to the group of desks, sat, and unfolded the note. It was one of those moments when you realize you've made a big mistake, it's too late to take it back, and you want to curl up and die.

"What's this?" He walked back down the aisle and stood by me.

I began to perspire. "Oh, th-this," I stammered as

though it were my mother's grocery list instead of the precious love note I had cherished and guarded for so long.

"Why did you put this on my desk?"

Good question. Why? My legs trembled.

Bobby looked closer, examining the crumpled paper open in his palm with the words *Do you love me?* and the yes box checked off, staring him in the face. "It's not mine."

I looked at him, confused. "This isn't your handwriting?"

"I wrote it," he said, "but for Daniel. Three years ago. We slipped it in the candy box before my grandfather sealed it."

"Oh, you remember." My voice drifted off.

"Yeah, I remember how shy he was. And still is." He handed the note back. "And Valentine's Day was yesterday if you're giving it to me now. Kind of late, huh?"

I looked over at Daniel, who was watching us. "Three years too late."

I slipped into my seat. My thighs stuck to the chair, sweat pouring through my tights. It took every last effort not to cry. *Be strong. Pretend. Act like nothing's wrong. I know there are terrible things that happen in the world, and on a scale of one to ten this is a zero.* But I couldn't help myself. This felt like a ten. I thought of the night when Daniel and I looked at the stars and he told me about black holes. *I wish that I could disappear into one right now.*

The rest of the day and the bus ride home felt forever. We passed my mother's school and I saw her on the playground clearing up paint supplies. She and a bunch of her students had been painting the jungle gym, and she had blue and orange streaks on her clothes. It was strange seeing my mother not being a mother, and instead, being a regular person, happy and separate from me and our family. *Should I talk to her?*

When I got home from school, I pulled down my shades, crawled under the covers, and stayed there until it became dark. And then I stayed there some more.

Matt knocked on my door and opened it without waiting for an answer.

"Go away. Can't you see I want to be alone?"

He stood by the edge of my bed and turned on the lamp by my night table. "Don't be afraid of the dark," he said, feeling my wet tears. He put his arms around me. His hair smelled of baby shampoo. "There are no lions and tigers and bears."

I put my arms around him. His cheeks felt fuzzy as a fresh peach, soft and innocent. I whispered, "I won't be afraid. I promise, little tiger."

And he cuddled under the blanket next to me. My seven-year-old brother was there.

Twenty-Four

Daniel

We're all human beings and we all make mistakes.
—Greg Louganis, diver and Olympic gold medalist

Patches of snow clung to dormant crocus bulbs, bulbs my mother had planted in October, before the earth hardened, before I went back to school. The tips of leaves were pushing through, waiting for spring, as she would have been impatiently waiting for them to bloom in her "mud and bud season." Presidents' Week came and went. She still hadn't come home. And I hadn't gone to see her. Neither had my father.

By March, therapy had been reduced to two days a week. On one of those days, I overheard Krista's mother say to her husband while I was coming into his office, "It's past the point of being a whim. How can a mother disappear like that?"

Mr. Harris answered, "I see all sorts of things during a crisis in my business. Health issues put a lot of pressure on the family and the marriage. We don't have that, and you know what we go through every day."

"She can opt out of a marriage but not out of being Daniel's mother."

"Fathers can mother."

"I know," she responded. "I also realize that I complain about all the work too, but I couldn't stay away for this amount of time; I love you and the kids too much. And especially a child like Daniel. At the beginning I kind of understood her, but now it seems so selfish. Could you imagine me leaving Matt or Krista after such an accident? I'd have to be certifiably nuts."

She looked stunned when she turned the corner and saw me in the waiting room. I pretended I was flipping through *Highlights* magazine to find the hidden pictures, but I'd have to be deaf not to hear what she said. "Oh, Daniel. Daniel. Daniel." She put her hand to her heart.

"It's okay, Mrs. Harris." I focused on the squiggly pattern on the carpet instead of her.

"No, it's not. I'm so sorry." She touched my shoulder. "I know your mother loves you. She called me before she left and asked me to keep an eye on you. She's not a bad person. She's searching."

I missed that kind of a touch. It was lighter than my father's heavy hand. *No, it's not okay. She said out loud what I felt. How could Mom leave? How could she not love me enough? Was she crazy? Searching for what?*

• • •

Krista seemed to be avoiding me too. Since Valentine's Day. I was going to erase that holiday off the calendar. We hadn't practiced swimming. It felt like a whole ball of hurt—like my mother's wool yarn before she made hats and scarves for us, knitting it into organized, straight, even rows that made sense.

The first day of spring break, I woke up to an empty house. Dad had left a note out on the island in the center of the kitchen under Mom's favorite mug. I poured orange juice into the mug as I read it. *Had to run to the law library for a new case. Will be back in a few hours. If you need me, call my cell. Lots of love, Dad.* On the floor was a pile of clean laundry in the basket, and I began to fold the clothes as I waited for the milk to boil for my oatmeal. I smiled at the size of my brontosaurus T-shirt compared to my father's old college sweatshirt. I turned on the radio and switched from station to station. A rap came on that Bobby had played at his party. I felt flushed and embarrassed about how Krista had given me the silent treatment. As I switched stations, I heard an announcer shout, "For all you crawdaddies out there, I've got a new group of gals hotter than jalapeño poppers: Jumpin' Jambalaya." I turned up the speakers until the bass thumped real loud, and tried to do my version of *Risky Business* in boxers instead of Jockey briefs, dancing and swaying with a walker everywhere—the kitchen, the hall, the family room, until the house was one big dance floor. I stayed on the station, song after song, until I turned the bass down a bit and the treble up during

"Swamp Mama's Waltz"—one written by the lead bass player. At the end, the radio guy added, "Sitting in on the recent recording session was our own newcomer, Emmaline Rosen. A little lady from way up North with a big Southern sound. And for you folks out there who think someone above the Mason-Dixon can't hold the line, she plays a mean fiddle. So get on your boots and cowboy hats for some fine stomping two-step."

The telephone rang, jolting me. It was someone trying to sell our family a monthly meat plan. So I told them we were vegetarians, and they hung up on me faster than an alligator eating a Double Whopper at Burger King.

When the phone rang a second time I was annoyed. "Yeah?" I said, about to hang up.

"Your mother was on the radio," Krista yelled into the receiver.

There was an extra beat of silence.

"Well, isn't she great?" she screamed with excitement.

"I guess," I said, sounding flat and unemotional.

"Is that all you can say? Aren't you listening?" she said, out of breath.

"Krista, my mother sent the CD. I've heard her already. Take in some oxygen."

"Okay, then," she said with a tinge of sarcasm, probably not knowing what else to say.

"There's something I want to do." I changed my tone. "And I could use your help."

"What?"

"Come and find out."

When she got to my house, I was dressed and holding the little tank filled with aqua pebbles, a palm tree, and our class frog, which I'd gotten to watch once again. "I woke up this morning and knew what I had to do."

She cocked her head to one side. "What's that?"

I looked at the tank. "Let the frog go."

"Are you sure about this? What about a class vote? Bobby said no."

"Who made him boss? And it was your idea."

"Actually, it was my brother's friend with his turtle," she said with new doubt in her voice. "And he's only seven. So what does he know?"

"I know, but I got to thinking. So I called the Science Center. An instructor got on and she said that it could live in the pond in the spring. Our frog could host mud-wrestling parties. Lily-pad leaps. Have new life experiences. We can visit, like you told us. There's no turning back."

Krista nodded, still looking somewhat doubtful.

We got on a bus that took us a short distance to an old mansion that had been donated for use as a science learning center. Leaves and twigs floated on the surface of a pond, waiting for spring cleanup. At first I held the tank and didn't want to let the frog out. My hands trembled as I took off my makeshift aluminum-foil, hole-punctured lid and eased the cube into the water. Krista covered her face and peeked through her fingers as the frog sat frozen on a leaf. Then it suddenly jumped high, flipping in a circle like a helicopter and disappearing under a fern frond. We knelt next to the marsh grass to search for our lost frog. Then it hopped, creating a ripple as it skimmed the clear, still, glassy surface. As I leaned over to scoop it up, I lost my balance and nearly fell in the pond, but a smooth stone broke my fall. The knees of my jeans got wet right through to my skin, though. Krista pulled me back by the sleeve of my jacket. "Are you trying to drown us?"

I imagined myself slipping away from the edge of the pond as it dipped deeper and deeper past reeds yellowed and dry from the long winter.

"Mr. James is going to kill us," I said, holding the empty tank with its palm tree.

"So is the rest of the class," she added.

"Look at you. You're a mess." She stared at my dirt-caked sneakers.

"You look pretty bad too." I picked at straw stuck to her hair and ribbed sweater.

We started cracking up and swung our arms out in a full circle in the field, shouting, "Freedom!" Then we walked back on the spongy lawn to the main entrance of the building. I gave the receptionist an envelope filled with our data. I was soaked and full of happiness and sorrow. The frog had beaten me to swimming on its own, but I wasn't done yet. I had a lot left in me.

Toward the end of the week Bobby called me. "The pool's heated. Your pass is officially valid. Like I promised," he teased. "Tomorrow after six sound good? My parents are going to a neighbor's for dinner, so we can hang out."

"Sounds great," I said. I wasn't going to check in with my father for approval. If he was home by then and asked where I was going, I'd blow him off and say I'd be at a friend's. When he pressed me, which I knew he would, I'd say the truth. And he'd have to accept it.

The next day when it was time to head over to Bobby's, Dad was out, so I called for a cab and paid for it with some of my allowance. I heard the speakers turned up real loud by the pool. When I got to the backyard, Bobby waved to me from the diving board. Steam evaporated off the surface of the water in the cool night air. Bobby jumped into the deep end while I waddled in like a seal off the starting block. The temperature was as warm as my bathtub. Suddenly my leg hit something hard, giving me a cramp. Was it the pool's vacuum, the long tube snaking around like an invader from space? I saw the top of Bobby's blond head in front of me. The closer I swam toward him, the farther he drifted, doing his laps, not noticing. I saw his legs kicking furiously, lit by underwater spotlights on both sides of the pool.

"Bobby!" I cried over the radio blasting on the patio. Could he hear me?

I treaded, gasping for air, looking in his direction. My eyes burned from the chlorine as I tried to get closer to the shallow end. I pushed on. There was a terrible ache in my calf all the way down to my toes, which were in spasm and bent back. I could barely breathe from the pain. I choked, spitting out water. Panicked, I tried float-ing on my back as Bobby did his laps, his head mechani-cally in and out of the water. *Please, God, if you're there, give me strength. I'll be good. I'll do anything.*

Bobby lifted his face and saw me. I sort of remember him dragging me back toward the shallow end, pulling me like the yellow duck float that was bobbing near the diving board. Back to the stone-and-cement steps, scrap-ing my arms and legs. Back to the brittle grass, first sprout-ing with the April rains. Back to life. Or did I imagine it? Because I must have blacked out for a few seconds. When I came to, he was performing mouth-to-mouth like Coach had taught us in first aid. We had barely paid attention, because who thought we'd ever need it? He called 911 when my lips turned deep purple and wouldn't stop quiv-ering as I lay under the three layers of towels. Then he called his parents. And my father, while an ambulance brought me to the hospital.

When I saw Dad in the emergency room he ran to my side and put his head down next to mine, his teeth chat-tering like those crazy fake teeth Brandon would wind up for Halloween parties. Trembling, he held my hand as though he would never let it go. Parents seem to belong to the same club. Once they know you're safe, they hug you, holding you tight until you're limp—like a rag doll, and they begin to let go and when they think you're not looking, they cry. My father did all of the above and then added his own next stage. He didn't really have to say a word to me because his expression said it all. *Were you out of your mind? What made you do such a stupid thing?*

When I stopped shivering from the shock of it all, I said with attitude, "I knew what I was doing. You've gotta trust me."

He gave me a look that said, *Oh, yeah, sure. I'm gonna trust you? In your dreams, kid.*

Parents think they have all the answers, but I have some answers too. Like the day of the fire drill when I helped Lainie and got the tadpole, I just acted. And that's the way I had to be even though Coach told me not to be such a hero. Because taking risks in life makes you grow. If you always play it safe, how do you change? How else do you stretch toward your dreams? Isn't that what I did by swimming at the Y with Krista? And telling her at Bobby's party I liked her? And signing up for the May Meet? And wasn't that what Bobby did to make things right, by asking me to come over and swim without our parents getting in the way? That's what we needed to do, so we did it. When I leaped into the deep end of the pool in his backyard, I didn't just leap for me. I leaped for Krista, I leaped for Bobby, I leaped for my father, and I leaped for my mother.

While I waited with my dad for the doctor on duty, the swim played over and over in my head. As the night wore on, the truth sank in: I could have drowned. And Bobby Kaufman had saved me.

"You're staying overnight for observation," the attending doctor told us.

"Do I have a choice?" I asked, terrified, not wanting to be in a hospital ever again.

"No," she said. "Actually, you don't."

My mother was by my side in the morning when I woke up. My secret wish all along had come true.

Twenty-Five

Krista

*Life is like an onion: you peel it off one layer at a time,
and sometimes you weep.*
—Carl Sandburg, poet

Easter decorations of origami rabbits were pinned to corkboards on the walls of the pediatric pavilion. I watched meal trays stacked on metal racks roll by in the hall through two swinging doors marked PATIENTS ONLY. I got a lump in my throat as they swung closed and I could no longer see where Daniel might be.

"Visiting hours begin in a half an hour," said a nurse at the front desk.

"My father works here in physical therapy. He dropped me off before his rounds."

She looked up from a chart and smiled. "Now twenty-nine minutes are left."

I guess her rules were different from Bobby Kaufman's grandfather's.

I headed straight for the gift shop in the atrium off the lobby. "Can I have that one?" I pointed to a balloon.

A friendly old lady with pearls and a VOLUNTEER tag on her cashmere button-down sweater slipped a deep-blue one out of the bunch. It had tiny silver stars. I paid for it and headed back upstairs.

Cartoons were blasting on TV's as I got off the crowded elevator on the pediatric floor. I passed a ward, then several double rooms—many with four patients crammed in, sharing—pretending to know exactly where I was going so no one would stop me this time. When I approached a private room, I thought I heard Daniel's voice. There was also the low mumble of a woman's voice, sounding strained. Trying to decide whether to go in or not, I held my breath in the hall as the woman inside let out a loud sigh. "I couldn't help it," she said. "I was drowning."

The word *drowning* hung in the air.

"While you were, you know"—she paused—"in the hospital, I tried to keep it together. And after, when you came home. But when you went back to school and things seemed okay, that's when I had a chance to finally think, and my life really began to fall apart."

"When did this become about you, Ma?"

There was a long silence. Should I tiptoe away? I felt glued to the wall.

She let out another deep sigh. "I want you to understand because I know you're mad at me and it tears me up inside to see you so full of anger. These last months, I've been allowing myself to just be. Some people might see that as weak. Others might consider it an unthinkable act—to leave you. But to me," she said, her voice cracking to a place so sad, "what happened was a catalyst to re-examine life. I know now I would have left if there had been no accident. It was just a matter of time."

My knees got weak as I listened. I sank to the floor outside Daniel's room.

"Sometimes"—her voice became barely audible—"when you were a baby and we first moved to Queens, early in the morning, before you and Dad got up and he left for work, I'd throw a coat over my nightgown and drive to the park under the Whitestone Bridge. I'd sit in the car with a thermos of coffee and stare at the city skyline, wanting to escape. Then at night, I'd dream of walking across the bridge, and in the dream I feared that if I took one step the wrong way, I'd fall in. And I had to face that fear—that things aren't always in your control. I guess I fell in. As the bumper sticker says, stuff happens."

"Tell me about it," said Daniel.

I heard the bed creak, and I nearly jumped up. I imagined she was hugging him because it grew very quiet.

"I love you, Daniel. I'm so glad I flew up here to be with you."

"Were you scared when you heard?"

Did Daniel have to do this to get her attention?

"I was terrified," said Mrs. Rosen. She began to cry. "It was such a foolish thing—to swim at night with no supervision."

"But you know I have to do things too, take chances, to prove myself, not just you."

"You could have drowned. The idea of living in a world without you . . . I couldn't." The words got caught in her throat. "You bring endless joy into my life. You are a part of me."

"What about Dad? Isn't he a part of you? You left him too."

"I went away, but *you* never left me. And your father is always here inside too. Maybe I had to let go to make room for something else? To realize what is missing."

"You sound like Coach."

What Daniel's mother said spoke to me. Maybe I'd have to finally let go of Bobby to make room for something else, and to realize what was missing all along.

"I need you. Dad needs you."

"I need you both too," she said.

Daniel began to cry as well. I swallowed, gulping tears down my throat until I felt empty.

Bobby and his father were heading down the hall toward Daniel's room. I felt trapped. I rose up off the floor and the three of us stood there with my balloon bobbing between us. "He's in there with his mom," I said.

"Oh," they both said, sounding uncertain about what to do.

Mrs. Rosen must have heard our voices, because she came out into the hallway. Her lips tightened into a fierce downward turn when she saw Dr. Kaufman. He gave her a strained smile and put out his hand, but she stood with hers rigidly by her side.

"I'll come back later," I said.

Mrs. Rosen reached out and took me by the wrist. "No, stay."

Bobby waved to Daniel from the hall. His father looked down and stuffed his hands in his pants pockets. Daniel smiled and waved Bobby inside. He gave Daniel some magazines and a paperback. They knocked their fists against each other. "Just wanted to see how you were," I heard Bobby say.

"Thanks. They're probably releasing me later today."

Bobby pulled the curtain so we couldn't see them. Mrs. Rosen paced the hall and Dr. Kaufman whistled nervously. Minutes passed in tense silence. Finally Mrs. Rosen blurted out. "*My* son's lying there, again, in a hospital bed—not yours. I've been doing this dance of hope. I want to go way past hope. I want my son back to the way he was."

Dr. Kaufman folded his arms across his chest.

Then she lashed into him. "How do you know you didn't make a mistake? Or a wrong decision? Do you know for sure that it wasn't *your* fault?"

"Is anything one hundred percent?" he asked her.

Her eyes seemed wild. "Yes. A child. Your mate, your life—those things can change, but your child will always be your child. I blame you."

At first he said nothing, and then he said with some difficulty, "I'm sorry."

"Too late," she said. "Sometimes a person needs to hear it at the time."

I glanced over at Mrs. Rosen. "It's never too late."

They both turned to stare at me. Mrs. Rosen's eyes

filled with tears, as did mine, and she draped her arms around my neck. Dr. Kaufman placed his hand on my shoulder, and then took it away as quickly as he had put it there. I remained in the hallway with both of them, holding this stupid balloon.

Finally Bobby came out. He smiled at me and said, "He told me everything."

"Told you what?" My heart raced.

"About the frog. That you both let it go."

"We all do dumb things."

Bobby bit his lower lip, gave me a wave good-bye, and walked off with his dad down the hall.

Mrs. Rosen looked upset. "I'm going to grab something to eat. Go in and see Daniel."

Dr. Kaufman, Bobby, and Mrs. Rosen waited for the elevator, and before she got in she put her hand on Bobby's shoulder. Dr. Kaufman smiled at them both.

I went inside and tied the balloon to a metal bar at the end of Daniel's bed. Daniel smiled and said shyly, "Guess you were a better swimming teacher than Bobby."

I fumbled with the balloon string. "It's nice Bobby came this time. And his father too."

"You know, Bobby and I never wanted to stop being friends. Our parents made us stop. They didn't have to see each other every day in school. It was easier for them."

I thought of Dr. Kaufman and Mrs. Rosen in the hall, so cold to each other. *Easy?*

"It's made it harder on us. I needed Bobby, and he needed me."

"I can see that. It's not always easy to forgive, is it?"

"What's easy?" he said.

We listened to rain splatter against the large picture window.

"Won't see the stars tonight," Daniel said with a smile.

I untied the dark blue balloon with the tiny stars all over it. It swirled upward. "Yes, you will," I said as it bobbed on the ceiling.

Daniel smiled, looking upward.

Dad drove me home after he was done seeing his patients. We went past stores on the wide boulevard twinkling with blinking lights and signs announcing holiday sales. "Is Daniel going to be okay?" I wondered out loud.

"He's in good hands."

"You think he's going to get all better?"

"All better?" he repeated.

"There's so much he still can't do."

"And there's a lot he can. He's come a long, long way in a short time."

"*Short* time?"

Dad cleared his throat. "I had a friend in high school, Anne, who was born without arms. Her mother had taken a drug called thalidomide, prescribed by a doctor while she was pregnant. They didn't know at the time it could have an effect on the baby."

I was quiet as I listened.

"After I got to know Anne, I never felt sad being with

her. She was smart and funny, and sat across from me in art class."

"Art?"

"Anne painted by holding a brush in her mouth." Dad drifted as though remembering. "Our teacher told us to go see nature. Anne loved the butterfly exhibit in the museum, so she and I went. The monarchs stayed on us and we couldn't leave because they wouldn't fly off. It took a while to figure out it was my tweed jacket they were attracted to, not me. And I desperately wanted to leave. Sue Sherman, editor in chief of the school newspaper and head of the cheerleading squad, showed up, and I thought that Anne would cramp my style." He looked down, seeming ashamed, and I thought of the times I felt that way with Daniel.

"Do you know what happened to Anne?" I asked.

"She became an artist," he said.

I gasped.

"I know," said my father. "Sometimes I think I became a physical therapist because of Anne. So to answer your question about Daniel, the strength of the human spirit is an incredible thing. Daniel will be all better in whatever form that takes."

That night, I dreamed of Daniel flying. Not on a plane, but past the moon—like E.T. on a bicycle or Peter Pan above the rooftops with Wendy. Flying to another place. A better one.

Twenty-Six

Daniel

Live all you can; it's a mistake not to.
—Henry James, author

Our first meal home together was major weird. Mom was touching objects in the kitchen as if they were old friends. She picked up her coffee mug—the one that had a heart and I LOVE MOM on it by its ceramic handle—and caressed it, and she smoothed her fingers across the flower design on the front of a plate that I had hand-painted when I was four. Then she watered all her plants. The succulents were still alive, the others dead and thrown out. When our neighbor across the way put his newspapers in the recycling bin and waved to her through the kitchen window, like old times, she let out a whimper like Bobby's dog, Max. Dad stood behind her by the kitchen sink. I remembered when he'd pick up her long hair and kiss her on the back of her neck. This time he didn't. She held her breath, as I sometimes did when I swam underwater. He said to her, "We have to get into our rhythms again." But my mother couldn't seem to get back into hers, or ours. So my father suggested, "Let's get into yours. Let's go to Louisiana for the rest of spring break." Mom smiled.

Before I knew it, we were in the Big Easy. I found several postcards in a store near Jackson Square in the French Quarter of New Orleans—one that hadn't been destroyed by Hurricane Katrina. The owner was so grateful we were tourists here on vacation that he gave me a half a dozen extra. I mailed them to Krista one at a time.

Dear Krista,
Heard you got snow in New York City! Ate gumbo, jambalaya, and boiled crawfish at a cookout-my mother's bandmates showed me how to rip the heads off and suck out the guts. Gives a whole new meaning to gross. Had chicory coffee and fried pastry called a beignet. Tell Gina it tastes like Nonna's zeppoles.

    Your partner in crime,

                    Daniel

P.S. Our frog better be okay in that spring snow! Talk about April showers!

Dear Krista,
Music everywhere! On street corners. In parks. Even a town square near a cemetery where famous jazz musicians are

buried! My parents did the two-step to music from a concertina-like an accordion. I was <u>so</u> embarrassed-they were the only ones dancing. When it was done, my mom played a song she wrote, "Bayou Blues." A crowd started building up and danced as she fiddled.

Hope you are having fun too.

Daniel.

Before I went to sleep in the hotel, I wrote another postcard—one I bought at the Aquarium, which had been repaired and restocked with new fish and animals.

Dear Krista,
Walked through a see-through tunnel filled with exotic fish and stingrays. Reminded me of our tadpole and its tank. There are penguins-Satchmo and Voodoo-they made it through the hurricane with the help of a police officer who had lost his home and lived in the aquarium. He babysat them after the storm when the generator blew. I watched them slide on their stomachs into the water the way I head into a pool. For now. Got a surprise for you. Don't get too excited. It's tiny.

Daniel

On the front I drew a scuba diver on the photo of the tank and labeled it "me."

The following morning turned above eighty-five degrees, so we headed out of the city on Highway 90 and drove very, very far for hours along the Gulf Coast. A lot of the houses and buildings were empty on the way—people who hadn't returned after the hurricane. We wound up at a beach where Dad had heard there might be an old shipwreck. My parents found a shack near the beach and rented some snorkeling gear. I tugged at the rubber reef slip-ons—a tight fit—as Dad picked out a tube with a mouthpiece my size. "Can I do this?" I asked.

Before he answered, I said to myself, *I think I can.*

When we got to a small cove with calm aqua water, my father parked the car and announced, "The Rosen Snorkeling School is officially open. And I don't mean a school of fish." I groaned. So did my mother, which was her way of saying she liked his little joke. He put my walker in the trunk and carried me across the sand like he'd done when I was little. "All you have to do is float on your stomach. Those sea creatures will do the rest!"

Mom watched us from the beach towel. She stood up, sat down, and then stood up again, looking fearful as my father and I swam slowly. He held my hand firmly as he pointed to striped, dotted, and multicolored fish with his free hand. The sandy bottom suddenly dipped deeper into a reef and I thought of the time I nearly lost my balance in the pond with Krista, but here I floated suspended above this unreal world. *I* became a fish. Or as Mom might say, very Zen-like, "*At one* with the fish." We saw an underground cave near the coral and I tossed Fruit Loops to swarms of iridescent blue and salmon-pink fish that swam past me. Then I came up for air, and we headed back.

My mother squinted in the blinding sunlight. "How was it?" she asked, looking relieved that I was back in one piece on dry land.

"I'll take you out."

"I don't know about that," she paused, looking over at my father questioningly.

I took her hand. "It's way beyond cool."

My father nodded as if to say, *I'm here.* "It'll be fine."

I adjusted my equipment, spitting on the face mask to prevent it from fogging up. My mother imitated me. Then after she helped me into the water, I held her hand confidently, not letting go. I felt her tension in the tight-ness of her grip. We paddled slowly away from the shore. In the distance, as the sun's rays gleamed, lighting up this underwater world, was a stream of jellyfish, glisten-ing like shooting comets, luckily heading in the opposite direction. We eased around several bright yellow-and-purple fish that I would have sworn under oath were smiling like clowns. Then I let go of my mother and she let go of me. We swam back alongside each other like two fish.

As the heat of the afternoon sun began to get unbear-able and my back started to burn, we packed up and headed to the car. We found a smokehouse on the road, a broken-down barbecue place that had ribs and fresh corn still in the husks, which we ate on the side of the road, licking our fingers. Hot and tired, the three of us remained quiet as we drove along the highway. We had finally found our rhythm.

Past dwarf palmetto, mimosas, and moss-laden bald cypress trees, I was excited to be in the world where my mother grew up. As the sun set, we headed on a very long drive to Aunt Edna's cabin, which she'd bought as a vacation spot with the small inheritance their mother had left her. It was out by a bayou filled with snakes and alligators. Her one-room bungalow was a shotgun-style house with a tin roof. It was built on stilts to avoid flooding, and I looked up at these pilings as if I had to climb Mount Everest. Underneath were stored a canoe and a rowboat with an outboard motor.

When I looked at the front door, I could see my aunt waving straight through from the back. I didn't recognize her at first. "Out back," cried my aunt, waving us to a long wooden plank from the yard to the door. Dad helped me along the steep incline. My walker thumped with each step up the makeshift ramp to the inside.

"Been a long time, *chéri*," she said affectionately, as she hugged me. I felt stiff in her arms. It had been a few years since I had seen her. I also needed my walker to hold on to. I wasn't sure if this was the coolest place I had ever seen, or my mother's younger sister was crazier than she was, being out here all alone.

A fly-studded strip barely waved in the damp and heavy breeze. Aunt Edna whisked bangs from her forehead, using a wooden spoon to stir the contents of a large black kettle on a wood-burning stove. I noticed Mom's violin case in the corner, and wondered what the humidity would do to the wood she had oiled with a special varnish and cared for so regularly.

"So." My mother stood there, with the same impish smile as her sister.

"Why don't you two take a little walk? Stretch your legs a bit from all that driving. Gives me time to catch up with my nephew here." Edna raised her eyebrows mischievously. "And the roux will have browned for my gumbo."

My mother looked at my father, and he nodded. "You'll be okay?" he asked me.

What could I say? *Oh great, you're leaving me alone with some relative I don't really know even though she's Mom's baby sister.* My mother gave me a squeeze before they left. I forced a smile as I looked around the room whose slatted walls had been hastily brushed with white paint. Shelves lined them, full of glass jars of jams marked huckleberry and blackberry and preserved vegetables labeled snap beans, okra, carrots, and turnips, from her backyard garden, with dates on the metal lids.

"Want a pickled turnip?" She saw me eyeing her bounty.

"No thanks." I smiled politely, afraid of getting food poisoning.

"Good. You'll save room for my gumbo."

I watched her stir, humming to herself as she measured out rice and red beans into a cup.

"Sorry about the accident," she said outright. She stared at my walker next to the caned rocking chair I was sitting on. "Real shocked at the news. But you seem to be holding your own."

I was taken aback at her directness.

"Not a talkative one, are you?" She handed me a warm biscuit and a glass of iced tea. Then she plucked a sprig of mint off a potted plant on the windowsill and stuffed the leaves in my glass without asking.

I took a sip. It felt cool in the heat.

"Your mom kind of raised me—being that we're sixteen years apart, and Mama got sick and died real young. Your mama liked to call me 'the caboose baby.' Our younger brother was stillborn, so I was the last child in the family."

I ripped off a piece of the biscuit and took a bite as I listened to family history.

"You can't have that without fresh sweet butter." My aunt slid a glass-covered dish across the table. "Yup, I was her first baby, kind of." Aunt Edna winked at me. "And she didn't seem angry about having to raise her own sister. Except when I started dating and staying out real late." She smiled to herself. "Now I'm the one who takes care of dozens of kids."

I looked at her questioningly, because I knew that she had none of her own.

She laughed. "I teach preschool."

I noticed green, pink, and blue-glazed plaster handprints

framing the window on the wall over the sink. We had one at home tucked away somewhere from when I was three.

"My treasures. From children who have no one to bring them home to." She stopped stirring, her spoon in midair, and stared at them like they were art in a museum. Sighing, she poured more iced tea into my glass. I was happy to get a refill because it kept my mouth full and that way I didn't have to make conversation. "As years go on, parents tuck these treasures away. But they should be out. A reminder of who that child was."

I looked at Aunt Edna, confused, wondering where this was heading.

"Your mother came back to revisit who Emma the child was. Sometimes you have to take a step back to go forward. She took care of me. She took care of you. Now she has to take care of herself for a little while. Maybe we should all just give her that chance."

I put the glass down on the wood table. The hand-hewn table wobbled. She tucked a folded piece of paper under the uneven leg to steady it and sat down next me. "I'm satisfied being a nursery school teacher. Your mother's ambitions were always greater. She got a scholarship to study classical music in Manhattan. That's pretty heady stuff for a young woman from here. And she never looked back. Until now. Her violin has become a fiddle again. And who cares what anyone calls it—a hog is a pig where bacon's concerned—as long as she plays. She's exploring. And is happy."

A small voice came out of my mouth. "What about me, Aunt Edna?"

She smoothed her hand across the knotted surface of the table in a small gesture, pushing the half-eaten biscuit toward me. "Have a little faith."

When Aunt Edna said that, I didn't take it like she was a Bible-belt nut job. I listened and took a small bite.

"It goes a long way."

I wanted to believe everything she believed. When I finished the biscuit, I got up and walked over to the window, resting my elbows on the ledge, listening to the budding sounds of the night—crickets chirping, frogs croaking, mosquitoes buzzing as they were coming out in droves at dusk. A nest with one fragile-looking pale blue speckled egg in the center was on the sill. It seemed waiting to be cracked open.

After my mother came back to the cabin, she began to rinse some greens in a colander. Her distinctive crescent-moon-and-star earrings twinkled in the dim glow of the oil lamp as she looked over at me. "I've got to tie up some loose ends before I head home."

My aunt saw my face fall. When my mother went out to my father on the back porch, Aunt Edna put a hand on my shoulder.

When I got home, after I unpacked my suitcase, I found a sealed envelope leaning against the base of the lamp on my desk with my name on it in my mother's handwriting.

Dear Daniel,
I've begun writing songs. Here's a bit of
one. You are my song.

                        Mom

Like twisted twine.
Like a leaf in the wind.
Like a rainbow that forms and fades.
Soar. It's your journey.
You are my heart. My soul.

A letter came days later.

My dearest Daniel,
It was wonderful snorkeling with you—
although I was scared to death!
    Now I know I can swim in dreams and in
life. Without falling.
    And so can you. And to me, that is most
important of all, Daniel.
    With all my heart,

                        Mom

I reread it several times, then jammed it into the
drawer alongside my loose change, rubber band ball,
pencils, and pens.

"How ya doing?" Dad asked as I looked up, closing
the drawer.

I shrugged.

"Yeah," he said, seeming let down too. He brushed his hand across my back.

Krista was waiting for me when I got to her house for some physical therapy.

I took a small package from my jacket pocket. "I thought of you when I saw this."

"You shouldn't have," Krista said as she unwrapped the present carefully, not ripping its gold paper. "A starfish!" She rubbed her fingers along each of its five sandy tendrils, extending like points of a star. She turned it over, smiling. "A star in the sea."

"I figured whenever you need the sky, all you have to do is look right in your hand."

"Once again, thanks, Daniel."

"Again?"

"Again. The valentine candy box. Now this. You've given me nice gifts. I have something for you also. Don't open it until you get home. Okay?"

"Whatever you say."

When I was done with the physical therapy session my father drove me home. I opened Krista's present—a container with a brand-new tadpole. A tag attached said:

> Mr. James is still going to kill us!
> So blame it on me. It was my idea.
> Sometimes it's nice to start over fresh.

Twenty-Seven

Krista

Man's main task in life is to give birth to himself.
—Erich Fromm, child psychologist

Sunday afternoon as I was finishing up the last bit of homework I hadn't done, the phone rang. "Krista?"

"Lainie? You're breaking up. I can't hear you. Where are you?"

"Coming back from the city on the train. Meet me at that tea place we hang out at—the one on Roosevelt Avenue where I get the red bean buns that I love when I'm not on a diet."

I had some math homework to finish, but there was something in her voice—a certain urgency to her tone. "Okay," I said. "Lain?"

"Yeah?"

"You're all right?" But her cell phone dropped the call.

I took the Q15 to Main Street and found Lainie sitting in the back of Shanghai Pastry looking sad. I hugged her. Hard. She was drinking iced bubble tea, poking at black balls of tapioca. I sat down opposite her and took a long sip of the cool foamy liquid from her glass.

"I was with my father, Stephan, at his loft in Tribeca over the weekend." Lainie sighed and swirled her straw in the tea. "I wish I could live with him. He took me to a gallery opening of his friend Briana's artwork in Chelsea. Afterward we had sushi, and then listened to a reading at a theater below the poetry bar KGB on East Fourth. At ten, we went to the People's Improv Theater, where we saw a sketch comedy show." She swiped at a small puddle with paper napkins she nervously pulled from a dispenser.

I listened, because what could I say? *I saw your father in action when he lived on our block. He never once drove carpool, mowed the lawn, or gave you my phone messages, and he missed most of the shows you were in where you were the lead.*

After that, we went our separate ways—me home to my parents and her to her mom. And I listened once more that night, when she wept into the receiver as I stood shivering with a towel wrapped around me after running out of the shower.

"I turned around when I got home, and left for my father's," she sobbed between gasps. It was the first time I heard her *not* call him "Stephan." She continued, "To escape *her*. My mother told me she made an appointment for tomorrow with a dermatologist to have my first laser treatment. She said, 'If your father's so great, go live with him and his new bimbo-of-the-month!' So I am."

"How long are you staying?" I asked. "What about school?"

"However long it takes. Maybe forever."

"Forever? Not forever, Lain."

Gina called the second I got off with Lainie. "We're ba-a-ck!" she yelled into the receiver, not knowing most of us had had Spring Break from Hell. "I'm gonna be a babesicle this summer whipping up frozen yogurt on the boardwalk at the Jersey Shore at my uncle's new place, Heavenly Whey."

"Gina, hold on a sec. Lainie split to her father's," I blurted out.

"Like Nonna always says, 'Family is like olives with pits. You love 'em, but sometimes you're in the mood for the ones stuffed with pimentos instead.' That's our Lainie, drama queen."

"No, Gina, I don't think so. Not this time."

"I leave you alone for a week and you've gone over to the other side?"

"There are no sides," I grumbled. "Just four different friends."

Before I went to sleep, I lay down next to my mother as she read in bed, listening to her breathe. "Lainie went to her dad's over the spring vacation and now she's gone back."

My mother sighed. "My heart goes out to Lainie's mother. It's not easy being a single mom with a twelve-year-old daughter. Hey, it's not easy being a married mother with a twelve-year-old daughter."

I tossed a pillow at her and she playfully tossed it back.

"How much do you love me?" I asked.

"To infinity."

"*Only* infinity?" I asked teasingly.

We snuggled in her bed for a few minutes.

When I went into my room, I pulled down an extra pillow from the top shelf in my closet and an old shabby shoebox fell on the floor. It was filled with scented stickers, trading cards, lanyards, and beaded bracelets from camp. I thought of the latrine at Girl Scout camp and shivered, vowing never to go back. I tiptoed into Matt's bedroom and left the box by his bed because he needed stickers more than me. Actually, I didn't need them at all anymore. Except for one. I took back an old one of Kermit the Frog and pasted him on the inside of my loose-leaf binder, thinking of him croaking, "It's not easy being green." Now I knew what he meant.

Monday morning, my chest felt heavy, like a meatball was stuck in it, as I waited outside homeroom, hoping Lainie had had a change of heart. She didn't show. I watched for Daniel too. He approached the classroom as Mr. James was writing a lesson on the board, his back to the class. Daniel's hands were shaking as he slid the tank on the bookcase under the frog chart. He and I looked down, acting busy, but taking in every move that Mr. James made. When Mr. James went to pull out a science textbook, he glanced into the tank. Daniel paled. Mr. James looked closer, then stood up, his eyes searching, until they rested on Daniel. I quickly went over to Mr. James.

"Yes, Krista?"

Daniel began to get up too.

Before he could come over, I admitted, "I bought a new frog because I let ours go free over the vacation. I'm sorry."

Daniel broke into our conversation. "I was the one who let it go."

Mr. James scratched his head. "Now I'm confused. You had the frog, Daniel, right?"

"Right." Daniel nodded.

"So it was your job," said Mr. James, "to look after it."

Daniel nodded a second time.

"But it was my idea to bring it to the Science Center," I said. "Actually, it was my little brother's idea."

Bobby walked over. "And a great one."

Mr. James put up both his hands. "All of you sit down. Clearly, we have a situation." Daniel and I sighed. "Both of you, outside, with me. The rest of you sit quietly and study."

The class groaned as we followed him into the hall.

He looked at us sternly. "You two took it upon yourselves to release the frog without asking me or the class. That wasn't fair."

"We're sorry," we said together, and did not even come close to mouthing "Jinx."

"Say you're sorry to your classmates. You'll both have to take care of the new one and buy its food. Twice a week, lunchtime, you'll assist me in the lab cleaning beakers, slides, test tubes, and the small animal cages. I don't believe in severe punishments, but I do believe in assuming responsibility for one's actions and owning up to one's deeds. In the end, you did that, but your actions were still wrong."

"I'm sorry," I said, gazing down at the floor tiles in the hall.

"Me too." Daniel sounded earnest.

"By the way," Mr. James added as we headed back inside the classroom, "over the summer I was going to take the frog, with the class's approval, to the center."

I whispered to Daniel when we got back to our seats, "Working in the lab sounds fun. What else can we do that will make him keep us in at lunchtime till June?"

He shook his head at me. "Mr. James doesn't know how much you love his lab. I could do better things with my time than clean mouse turds and fish gunk."

At lunch, Brandon wanted to know the gory details. When we were finished recounting what happened, he asked, "Is that it?"

Gina said with a straight face, "They're really being put on the rack, tortured, and sent to the dungeon under the cafeteria for three years, out in one if they're on good behavior."

"There's a basement under the caf?" Brandon asked her.

Daniel, Bobby, and I laughed. Bobby was wearing a new black T-shirt that was the same as Daniel's. It had AQUARIUM OF THE AMERICAS, NEW ORLEANS on the front with an emerald-colored frog. I was happy that Daniel had given me a starfish. When I got home from school, I spread the tissue paper out on my desk and once again felt its hard bumpy surface. It had once been alive and soft. I perched it on the ledge of my windowsill so I could see Daniel's star—my star—day and night.

The doorbell rang when I got home from school. It was Bobby. My head pounded seeing him standing there on my front stoop.

"Do you know if Lainie's home? She left a message on our answering machine that she'll be away a few weeks. There's no one at her house and she sounded strange."

I glanced through the screen door at Lainie's house across the street. The blinds and curtains were shut, and the car was parked in the driveway, so I figured Lainie's mother might be there. "Lainie had a knock-down, drag-out fight with her mother and left to cool off at her dad's for a while."

He winced. "That's not good."

I could see he felt bad for her. A part of me wished I could have invited him in, but he left as quickly as he came when he didn't find what he wanted—Lainie.

Lainie was back home in less than a week. "Stephan had to go to the West Coast to stage a performance piece at some contemporary museum and there was no one to stay with me other than Briana, who looks and acts the same age as me. I know I'm mature, but please." She forced a smile, but I could see the disappointment all over her face—the same kind I had seen on Daniel's about his mother letting him down. I could see her father was back to "Stephan." And I could see Lainie, the little girl with the ugly brown shoes, still waiting for party shoes, as she ripped up the postcard from her father's gallery opening, the pieces falling on her carpet like snow.

Twenty-Eight

Daniel

Life is truly a ride. . . . The ride is the thing.
—*Jerry Seinfeld, comedian*

My father yelled out, "Daniel, pick up. It's for you!"

"Who is it? I'm working!"

"Your mother."

"Hi, sweetie," she said cheerfully when I got on the phone. "Anything new?"

"Hi," I muttered. "You called me, so you tell *me* what's new."

"I have some good news and some bad news." When I didn't say which order I wanted them in, she said, "The good news is that I am going to be playing at Jazz Fest!"

"Okay. What's that?"

"It's in New Orleans, and it's a big deal that goes on for days. We aren't getting the main stage, but they're giving us a spot in the festival. Everyone who is anyone in this kind of music—zydeco, country, rhythm and blues—will be here. There's great Cajun and Creole food at booths on this huge campground and music morning till night. It goes on all over town, so we also got a gig at Rock 'N' Bowl, outside of the inner city in a strip mall. It's a bowling alley upstairs, with one band going on around ten until midnight, and a dance place downstairs with another band. We'll be the bar band. Upstairs. This is *really* huge for us."

"And what's the bad news?" I cut her off.

She let out a loud sigh. "Well, the festival is usually at the beginning of May, but this year it's the same weekend as your swim meet. I don't know what happened."

"Oh," I mumbled.

"Honey, I feel awful."

"Just like you tell me about the swimming, how can you pass up an opportunity like this? Go for it. There'll be more meets."

"Really?" She sounded relieved, as if I had given her permission to do what she had already decided to do.

"Sure," I lied.

This was the place for her to say, *There'll be more Jazz Fests and bar gigs, so I'll come to see you at the meet,* but she didn't. Instead, she said, "See you after we both blow them away. Reach for the moon."

"Listen, I've gotta go study for a big test." I put down the receiver without wishing her good luck because I was too choked up and angry. I threw a trophy across the room—the one I had won at a competition my mother had taken me to in Florida, when I placed first in the backstroke and second in the 100-meter butterfly. It sailed across the room, hitting the green-glazed handprint I'd made in preschool—the one I'd found on a shelf in Mom's studio when I came back home, and had hung over my desk—breaking it into two pieces. Then I began to dump my silver and gold medals into the wastebasket, and with each toss I yelled, "Let Bobby do trials for the Junior Olympics. Let Bobby win statewide championships and national titles. Let him practice with some fancy private coach from Squaw Valley. Let him win the May Meet." I opened my desk drawer, found the song my mother had written, and crumpled it into a ball. Then I went into the kitchen and threw all the trophies and the broken pieces of the handprint into the trash along with the song. I found a plastic plate I'd made for Mother's Day that said, I LOVE YOU, MOMMY and had stick figures of her and me. You couldn't break it if you were the Incredible Hulk, so I flung it like a Frisbee out the window. Her favorite ceramic mug followed. And last, I dug out Mom's keepsake box. I tore up all the cards I'd made for her birthdays and holidays and started a small bonfire in the backyard in a metal garbage can.

My father ran outside. When he saw what I was doing he grabbed a videotape that I was about to throw in the flames—of me swimming in the Guppy group at day camp when I was four, about three boring hours' worth of me splashing and waving at the camera. Mom cherished it and would watch it whenever she felt down, since it made her laugh. At the end was me imitating Yoda from *Star Wars* in my scratchy, high-pitched voice and then lowering it to try to sound like Darth Vader.

"What's going on?" Dad cried. He grabbed Mom's memento box, filled with my projects she had saved over the years, including a felt bookmark I had made with flowers pasted on her name and an IOU in my first-grade handwriting for Father's Day, "Good for One Back Rub." Then he ran and got the garden hose from near the empty window boxes that would have had morning glory and marigold seeds germinating if she were home. First he put out the fire in the can, and then he sprayed me lightly. "Cool down, Daniel."

I was totally unprepared and felt shocked that my father would do such a thing. I grabbed the hose out of his hand and sprayed him back. The two of us wrestled for the nozzle as we stood there like drowned rats—we must have been quite a sight. I didn't know whether to laugh or cry. We both started to laugh, I think, to save ourselves from crying. But when he hugged me against his chest, I couldn't stop myself from sobbing. All he could say over and over again was, "I know, I know, I know."

Disappointments. They're endless. I wanted the hurt to stop. To go away forever. Dad bent down and picked up the two broken pieces of my handprint. I found the lost chip. It fit into the edge. I handed it to him. "We'll glue it later," he said. Then we dried off inside and changed our clothes. Dad jangled his car keys in the air.

"I don't feel much like cooking tonight—although we could have a barbecue."

"Very funny, Dad."

It was warm and sunny, almost seventy-five degrees. If Mom were home, she'd be giving violin lessons, and the music would drift into the garden, where all her flowers and vegetables would be starting to sprout. It would be the beginning of things. She loved it when the world bloomed, and we loved being a part of her happiness. The kitchen, the garden, seemed too big without her presence. Mom filled it up.

"Yeah," I said to my father, "let's eat out. House of Heavies?" I teased, using the name we'd made up for the Pancake House, where my father loved to order a large stack of blueberry pancakes.

We passed the Kaufmans' house on the way. Dr. Kaufman's van was parked out front in the driveway with its vanity license plate: DR TOOTH. There were bikes scattered on the front lawn. I imagined Brandon and some of the guys from the swim team playing volleyball in his pool. I felt a pang that he hadn't invited me, but I understood his fear after our last swim. I figured that when they all went home, Bobby would train for the meet. He'd put in at least another three hours of swimming. I remembered when I'd done that on my own, with no one pushing me. I was always competing against myself to get to the next level, never being satisfied. Mom said artists are the same way; it's the nature of things to want more, to do better. Now, though, I'd be satisfied with not making a fool of myself when I swam at the May Meet. I had more good days than bad days, so I guessed I was doing pretty well. It felt like the accident had happened so long ago—almost a year of my life wrecked. Who would have thought that my personal goal would be to get rid of a walker? I was determined to achieve that goal before the meet.

I went into one of my physical therapy sessions, passing Matt, who was building a new World Trade Center on the floor of the waiting room. "How ya doing, big guy?" I asked, ruffling his shaggy brown hair.

He turned his face upward. "Fine," he said, and went back to the Lego tower.

I smiled to myself, remembering the endless tents Krista and I had made out of old blankets, towels, and sheets in her bedroom or mine when we were younger, graduating to appliance boxes in the summer and digging tunnels in the snow during winter.

Mr. Harris squatted beside me while I did leg lifts and I thought, *Now what?* He put his hand on my shoulder and looked me straight in the eye. "Well, buddy," he said with a grin, "it's time to put the walker out to pasture."

"You mean it?" I asked.

"Yeah, I believe you're strong enough. I wouldn't be surprised if all that swimming practice helped more than I did to strengthen these limbs of yours."

"I don't know about that." I knew how much Krista's dad supported me.

"Well, I do."

"Does that mean I won't be seeing you anymore?" I

asked, feeling nervous about being out there on my own, but at the same time looking forward to it—and also wondering if I would see Krista as much outside school if I wasn't going to therapy.

He must have seen the expression on my face. "Hey, drop by any time you want to. You can ease into it. I'm here if you need me. I'm not abandoning you."

I let out a deep sigh. "Good."

My father returned the walker to the surgical supply place the next day.

The morning of the May Meet was the first one in a long time where I didn't think of all the things I couldn't do. When I woke up I said to myself, *I know I can do this.* Then as the hour of the meet got closer, doubts set in. *Am I going to humiliate myself? Embarrass my father? Let Coach down?* As I got dressed to leave, the phone rang and I just knew it was my mother calling to wish me luck by the way Dad was standing and nodding, looking like he too was filled with disappointment. He gestured for me to come over, and I shook my head no. He held the receiver out further and pressured me with his look, without saying a word, so I took it.

"I love you, Daniel," my mother said at the other end. "I will love you no matter how you do today. Do you understand that? Just doing what you're doing is winning."

I didn't want to give her an inch to make her feel better, so I said nothing.

"Daniel? Are you there?" She must have heard me

breathing. "I'm not the best mother in the world, but neither am I the worst. I know you feel that I am, and right now I feel that too. I'm so sorry." And my mother broke down.

Suddenly, and I don't know where it came from in me, I broke down too.

"You don't have to say you love me back. I understand. I'll call later to see how you did. Okay, sweetheart? Be strong."

"Okay," I replied, which was my way of saying *I love you* without saying it.

Bobby was stretching and doing sit-ups when I came into the locker room.

As I jammed my stuff into the locker, Bobby said, "There's a terrific ten-year-old who's someone to watch out for."

"There's always going to be someone else coming up," I said with a shrug.

"It won't only be you and me." He smiled. "I remember when Coach first saw you swim. My heart sank to my feet. I knew by looking at my father's face that from then on I would have to work harder if I wanted to place in anything."

"Guess you don't have to worry about that anymore."

"Oh, I will," he said. "It's only a matter of time."

We bumped fists gently and said together, "Break a leg."

Coach came up to me before I went into the waiting

area next to the pool. "I'm so proud of you, Daniel. You worked hard this year at that physical therapy and everything else you did. I wonder if you know how much respect I have for all your effort."

My face turned red. "Thanks, Coach."

"I'm not putting you in a medley relay today because I think you'll be too tense about letting the team down if you're not as fast as you want. I don't want that for them, but most of all right now, I don't want that for you." He put his hand on my back. "You understand what I mean?"

I paused. "I understand. I probably would do the same thing if I were you, Coach."

Coach smiled. "There's going to be five events for different age groups. I'm putting you in yours—freestyle swim, twelve to fourteen." He gave me a squeeze on the arm. "Go out there and show me what you have."

The pool area had stadium seating. The bleachers were filled with grandparents, parents, and noisy kids. I tried to find my father's face in the crowd but couldn't. Part of me was glad my mother wasn't here because she might have made me more nervous. I felt terrified as I went over to sit with the other swimmers. Bobby was already perched on the starting block. A quiet hush filled the air waiting for him and the others in his race to dive. Some of the lights flickered over the enormous pool. Bobby smoothed his hands across his wet hair and put on a thin rubber swimmer's cap that had our school name on it and a small American flag. I silently rooted for him, and noticed his father pacing until the whistle finally blew. Students and teachers from our school stood up when Bobby won by a big margin, beating his own personal best from last year, but not mine. Even some parents from other schools rose with thunderous applause.

Then it was my turn. I wasn't totally used to walking without the walker on the wet tiled surface of the floor, so I gingerly stepped up to the starting block of my lane, hoping I wouldn't slip. Once again, there was a sudden, peaceful silence filling the hall until I heard some kid whistle from off to the side, "Go, Rosen!" The swim team from my school started to clap. Coach put his hands up and made them stop immediately. I turned around and looked over at him. He smiled, and then I composed myself again, raising both my arms. *Relax. Breathe in and out. Like when Mom does her yoga exercises.* In the old days, fifty or a hundred yards of freestyle would be a joke, but now, could I make the laps needed to finish with the rest? *Do your best,* I heard a voice in my head say. I focused on my toes curling at the edge of the platform. Then I glanced straight ahead of me across the lane and jumped, wiping out the audience like Mom did in a darkened hall when she played onstage. Just her and the violin. Only the music. As soon as I hit the water, all I could think of was me and the lane, nothing else. Nothing except the sound of filters and me knifing through the water.

When I was halfway, though, I suddenly felt how badly I wanted to finish like everyone else, and I tightened up from the stress. I squeezed my elbows together to get length in the stroke, but it didn't work. I lifted my head for a second and could see my team rise to their feet, cheering. I felt shaky and didn't think I could go on. *Concentrate, Daniel.* Then through my goggles I saw Bobby running toward my lane. He jumped in. Other members of the team followed him. In an instant it felt as though everything was in slow motion, like a movie. As I struggled to finish the last lap everyone on my team dived in and glided along with me, filling all the lanes in the entire pool. It must have been quite a sight from above in the bleachers. They messed up the race, of course, and no one won. As I got out of the pool, some parents from other schools who didn't know me were shouting, "No fair! Do over!" But most of the crowd stood up and cheered when they realized what had happened. Bobby, along with the rest of the team, threw his arms around my neck and helped me to the bench. There were no winners or losers. We all won together.

A few minutes later all my friends came down to congratulate me. Mrs. Harris held a tissue in her hand and handed one to my father, who sounded like a foghorn when he blew his nose. Mr. Harris looked joyful, as if he too had been swimming along with me. In a way, he had. Krista was rubbing her eyes, as were Sandy and Lainie. Even Brandon's and Gina's looked red. "You were amazing," Lainie exclaimed. "I feel proud that you're my friend," she added. "I know how hard it was."

Krista threw her arms around my neck and kissed me, and without thinking, I kissed her back. We looked into each other's eyes and knew. It didn't feel like a friend kiss. It felt like something more.

"No one's ever going to forget this." Coach shook his head in disbelief as he tucked my head in his huge forearm. "They'll be talking about this one for years. What a crazy bunch of kids you are!" he shouted to the team.

"You did it!" my father shouted with a wide grin.

"Well," I said, "with a little help from a lot of people."

My father hugged Bobby, who stood next to me. And he and Bobby's dad hugged too.

Matt gave me his "next-to-best sticker"—a laughing goldfish hologram. "It changes into a fierce shark when you tilt it a certain way, and it glows in the dark," he told me proudly.

A little later my mother called on Dad's cell. "I hate that I missed that! Tonight isn't going to be as rewarding without you guys here at the festival. Especially you, my sweet, sweet Daniel."

Dad told her, "It won't be the same as being here, but I got it all on tape," which must have made her feel better. Later he said to me, "And I'm making another copy and keeping it in the safe deposit box at the bank until your mother comes home. I'm not taking any more chances with your moods."

I played the sprint and the kiss over and over in my head a hundred times as I tried to fall asleep. I couldn't drift off, so I called Krista on the telephone.

"Congratulations!" she said again, her voice muffled—she probably had the receiver under her quilt, just like I did.

"But I came in last."

"Hey, it was chaos in that pool. No one came in last!"

"Thanks, swim buddy."

"For nothing, swim buddy," Krista whispered back, adding, "Barracuda."

And if you could hear a smile, I was smiling.

Twenty-Nine

Krista

Goodnight stars. Goodnight air.
—*from* Goodnight Moon, *by Margaret Wise Brown*

Sunday night I slept over at Sandy's because we were going to get up early to march in the local Memorial Day Parade that the Elks or Bisons or some group of wild boars was sponsoring. Sandy lent me her plaid drawstring pajama bottoms, and I gave her my favorite top from the Gap, the one that I couldn't part with, but I could for her. It was bleached-out in one of my brother's attempts at the laundry, but it looked like something a hippie would have worn in the sixties. The cotton of Sandy's pj's felt soft against my skin, like the old flannel baby blanket that I'd slept with until it was in pitiful shreds. I still had a tiny gray swatch of my nappie left in the back of my pajama drawer.

Sandy and I got under a crocheted afghan, watching movies as raindrops beat down on the roof. Eric kept walking by, and we'd giggle as he grabbed a Twizzler from the large jar we were sharing. Sandy looked at me with bits of red between her front teeth and said something that sounded like, "Wot?"

I smoothed my tongue over mine, licorice stuck in them too, and said, "Nuting."

I thought of when Daniel had stopped being friends with me and I had wondered who would be honest enough to tell me if I had a poppy seed stuck in a tooth. I had room for many friends. Many *different* kinds of friends. It would be boring if they were all one type.

I looked over at Sandy. "Was it okay with you that I kissed Daniel?"

"We were all flipping out for him. Everyone was kissing. It was just a kiss, right?"

"Right," I said. But I thought to myself: *Number seven: Kiss a boy on the lips.*

After the holiday weekend, no one wanted to return to school. June meant end-of-the year testing, report cards, and finding out who your teachers would be for the next year. It was a sweltering day. How come *only* the main office, the nurse's office, and the teachers' lounge were air-conditioned? Weren't *we* slaving away?

While Daniel was being congratulated by Ms. Bean, our principal, in her office for his swimming feat, I collected money to have pizzas delivered from Angelo's during lunch to Mr. James's classroom while Gina placed the order.

"Here's extra money for drinks." Mr. James handed me a twenty to put in the pot.

When the delivery boy showed up at the door of our classroom with a stack of large, grease-stained white pizza boxes, no one was surprised except Daniel.

"What's this?" he said when I lifted the lid to one of the boxes and he saw his name spelled out in anchovies with a second line saying, NUMERO UNO.

Gina stared innocently at the flaked paint on the ceiling as Brandon swallowed a slimy fish. He grimaced as he realized what he'd eaten and gagged as if he'd swallowed a slug. "Who thought this up?"

"No comment." Gina looked at me and then at the ceiling again.

"At least they put on 'the works.'" I picked off an anchovy from my slice and tossed it onto Gina's piece. She gobbled it down.

"It was symbolic. Daniel swims like a fish," she insisted.

I rolled my eyes.

"It was the best I could do on such short notice. Anyway, my family loves them," Gina said with pride. "And they're great in a Caesar salad."

I gave her that whatever-you-say look because there was no arguing with Gina, but I was relieved that I was finally doing something I should have done at the beginning—giving Daniel a pizza party.

Uncle Carmine showed up with his new yogurt

Dream Pies and tubs of Lemon Zest and Tutti Frutti. Mr. James scooped seconds from containers into small paper Dixie cups, and thirds for Brandon, who tried all three. Gina helped her uncle. "Building those arm muscles in preparation for my summer at the Jersey Shore, where I'll be scooping from dawn to dusk for busloads of cute guys."

"Make sure you wear something sexier than those fatigues," Lainie said to Gina, whose face began to tighten until Lainie added, "I can lend you my sundress." Lainie smiled at me, hoping Gina would accept her offer.

When the bell rang ending lunch, we rushed to clean up. Mr. James told us, "We've been invited to the Science Center next week. Have your permission slips signed and bring a bagged lunch for an outdoor picnic with a special friend."

"What do you mean?" Brandon asked. "Who?"

"You'll see." Mr. James wiggled his eyebrows up and down like Brandon.

The following week was even muggier. Lainie showed up for the class trip in a red halter top with her hair pinned up, her tattoo showing. There wasn't a girl in the class who didn't gather around to examine it, asking if it hurt getting it—all the grisly questions we had wondered ourselves. She also wore bronze glitter on her high cheekbones. It wasn't a shock to anyone that Bobby sat next to her on the school bus as we headed toward the Science Center. It was something I'd learned to accept.

I sat next to Sandy, who was wearing her Girl Scout T-shirt from Camp Quidnonk from last summer. It was faded and too small. I guess she would buy a bigger one this year when she returned. I was so happy—not only would I never see my counselor, Enid, again, but my hair and clothes wouldn't smell like a burnt marshmallow for eight weeks. I knew I'd miss Sandy. She begged me to come back with her, but the thought of the latrines, the smell of Pine-Sol mixed with ammonia, having to clean pots after each meal, and no boys didn't entice me. I didn't ever want to rig a tent or see a sleeping bag again in my entire lifetime. Even when Sandy cried, "But we'd be CITs now! Together! We've waited years for this. How can I do it all alone?"

I looked off in the distance and admitted to myself, not to her, that I didn't aspire to be a counselor in training. What I said instead was, "I'll write every day. Promise. It will be as if I'm there. I'll hear your news. You'll hear mine. We'll be ecstatic when we see each other in August."

"But I'll miss you." Her eyes teared.

I couldn't tell her the truth, because although I didn't want to keep anything from her, I also didn't want to hurt her feelings. I had outgrown that camp like I had outgrown many things and I couldn't ever go back. Ever.

"Brandon's going to camp for the month of August," Sandy said, changing the subject.

Gina leaned over, awkwardly tugging at the spaghetti strap on one of Lainie's old sundresses that Lainie had lent to her. "He's going to drama camp, where he can write skits and act like the funny guy in plays, which shouldn't be too big a stretch. And they don't rough it at that camp. Think trailer parks with electricity and showers. Hotplates, not campfires like you'll be having. And trust me, he won't be missing any reruns of the *Simpsons*."

Before I had a chance to ask Lainie and Bobby what they were doing, we arrived at the Science Center.

The education director welcomed our class and took us on a tour of the center. We went up a wide, winding mahogany staircase into several different smaller rooms stacked with beakers, tanks, petri dishes, microscopes— you name it, they had it, from spiders to electric eels. I was in heaven, swooning as much as I used to when I thought of Bobby. (What did it say about Bobby Kaufman, putting him on the same level as an arthropod or bacterial culture?) The director said with the nicest smile, "Wander freely about the center. Take your time and enjoy. Our instructors are here to answer any of your questions. Please take a membership brochure on your way out."

As she turned to leave, I meekly approached her. "Do you have summer jobs for helpers? Like an intern?" I asked. "My science teacher, Mr. James, is right here and he could vouch for me. I worked for him these past few months." Of course I didn't tell her why—that I had freed a frog, one that was on these very premises. Somehow, I didn't think that would go over too big. She'd imagine black widow spiders running rampant, crawling along the wooden banister.

"Actually, we have a Junior Explorer Program for budding scientists your age. You can get a form downstairs in the office as you leave. Just fill it out and give it to the secretary. We'll be deciding in two weeks and let you know soon. It begins after July fourth and is three days a week. The other two we take children on outings or sleepovers in the museum at night to explore the stars and night creatures."

I was so excited I tugged at Daniel's sleeve like a little kid. "Did you hear that?"

"Yeah," he said.

"Want to do it with me?"

"I'm going to be swimming every day. Taking advantage of the hot weather. You could swim with me the other two days at the pool club outdoors."

"Swim buddy, if I get this job, I promise I will personally be your coach *and* cheerleader!"

Daniel smiled at me. "Or maybe I'll be yours."

We both realized this summer was going to be one of following our dreams.

After I carefully answered every question on the application, Mr. James promised, "I'll write a letter of recommendation." When I saw him give the education director a peck on the cheek good-bye and say, "See ya tonight. What should I pick up for dinner? Want to grill tuna? Or chicken?" I figured that I was in.

Mr. James led us down a slight hill toward the pond. He put picnic blankets out on the lawn. Then he told us to gather around the reeds fringing the edge of the water. He scooped up a frog with a net and cupped it in his hand. "There's been a record crop of frogs this year. We'd like to think that our class frog contributed to this new family at the Science Center." He looked at me and Daniel and winked. "I will miss this class not only because it was a bright one but because it was feisty, and I like that better than a perfectly quiet good one. You asked questions and challenged me. Lainie had asked at the start of the semester, does a lobster have lips? I don't know. I never kissed one, but I'll let you know after my trip to Maine this summer." Everyone laughed.

As we sat around, ate, talked, threw Frisbees, flew kites, and ate some more, I figured that Mom was right— people aren't all bad or all good. They are complex, with many hidden layers, some hidden even to themselves.

I glanced over and saw Bobby and Daniel off on the side together, kneeling near the swamp grass, deep in conversation. I wondered if they were looking for our frog. When Daniel came over, I said, "What's up?"

"Bobby just told me he's moving over the summer."

I felt a pang in the pit of my stomach, which I didn't know I would feel after all that had happened, but now the loss was definite, and forever. When people move, they say they'll come back and say hi, but they rarely do. It's what is.

"How come?" I asked casually.

Bobby surprised me when he spoke up from behind me. "My dad felt I needed to go further with my swimming. The private coach I have now could take me only so far. There's a man down in Florida who claims he can train me for the Olympics and put me on the map nationally."

"And you can swim outdoors year-round down there," I added. "It's always summer."

"Whatever," Daniel said, seeming dejected.

"Guess you'll miss the competition. Someone to egg you on," teased Bobby.

"Always thought I competed against myself. Maybe not entirely. I'll miss you. A lot." Daniel looked as if he was about to cry, and I could see him fighting to keep control of himself.

Bobby walked away, wiping the corner of his eyes as he went toward Lainie.

So will I, I thought. Then I looked over at Lainie and Bobby giggling on one of the picnic blankets. There are some girls who get guys like Bobby. And then there are some girls like me, who don't. They get to stay with boys like Daniel.

I thought back to what my mother had said about not needing diamonds because she had us—me and my brother and my father. Daniel is a diamond. No, I take it back—Daniel is an interesting stone like my mom's smoky green one. It has clouds. It is clear and dark and changes in the light. She says that it is imperfect and it has "character." And I like that better. I will never grow up and need diamonds.

After dinner I heard Lainie screaming at her mother through the open screen door and her mother yelling back at the top of her lungs. So things were normal again—for them. Lainie called when it got silent. "I'm moving in with my father for the summer. He might take me with his new girlfriend, Zoe, to some art biennial somewhere in Italy." I knew her father would find some excuse to dump Lainie and she'd be back in a week, which meant we'd have the summer to get to know each other even better. It was odd how we'd come to understand each other.

I went out to the backyard, looked up at the sky, and saw Orion's belt. The three stars pierced the sky. Daniel had told the class in one of his reports on the subject, which was almost as close to his heart as swimming, "In Roman mythology, Orion was the handsomest hunter of his race. The goddess Diana loved him, but he was accidentally killed and she placed him in the heavens as a constellation." He added, "When a star dies it still exists in the universe." My secret wish had come true—the one I had made the day Mom and I had lunch in the city and I had tossed the penny in the pool outside the museum. I'd wished for my own wishing star, one that I could cast endless hopes and dreams on when I needed to, because people have good things and bad things happen to them, and you can always use more than one star or one wish in a lifetime. I used to think that one of the stars of Orion's belt would be for Bobby, but not now. One would be for Lainie—she needed it more than anyone. One would be for Daniel, and one would be for me.

I imagined Daniel would wish for his mother to return. She was supposed to, and if this were a movie she would have shown up at the meet or the picnic or tonight and surprised him. Everything would be neat and tied up with a pretty pink ribbon. But I guess there are things you cannot grasp like a star. You can just dream and imagine. I closed my eyes and wondered what Daniel would become. I imagined something special.

When I came inside, I picked up the starfish Daniel gave me and looked up the word *starfish* in the dictionary. In the definition, the word *asteroid* appeared, "with five or more rays stretching out from the center—also called sea star." Oh, like orbits and planets and constellations. Then, several definitions below, I saw the word *stargazer.* It said, "an astronomer or astrologer, a daydreamer, a person who stargazes, and any of several marine fishes of the family uranoscopidae." I thought of Daniel's mom, and then of Daniel. I decided to hang around and see where Daniel's trip would take me, and where mine would take him. Each other's orbits. He taught me that nothing's impossible, and the true meaning of unconditional love. I think I'm going in for a second kiss.

Thirty

Daniel

*Hope lies in dreams, in imagination, and in the courage
of those who dare to make dreams into reality.*
—*Jonas Salk, scientist and inventor of polio vaccine*

The doorbell rang, and when I opened the door, I saw
Bobby with his dog. Max was wagging his tail.

"Wanna go for a walk?" Bobby jingled a rubber bone
as Max ran in circles.

"Max!" My voice rose as he tried to jump up on my
legs, sniffing at my crotch.

"No!" Bobby tugged him back with the leash.

I grabbed my keys, stuffing them into my shorts. We
ambled past houses half torn down on small plots, becoming construction sites for McMansions. "Who lives in
those things?" I said, shaking my head. "They're as big as
the church near our corner."

Bobby shrugged. "I don't know. Not people like us."

We walked past Twenty-fifth Avenue. As we glanced
up the block, the girls were hanging out on Gina's front
porch with Nonna. They waved, we waved back. No one

was playing games—pretending that we didn't know that they were there and them acting as if we were lawn gnomes. "See you later!" they shouted, and went back to whatever they were doing as we continued on our way.

We walked around a cove, the land jutting into the water under the Whitestone Bridge—my mother's bridge. A faint crescent moon and sun were in the sky at the same time, reminding me of my mother's earrings and our trip. When I looked one way, I could see the Bronx; the other way was the glow of the Manhattan skyline. I imagined my mother sitting in her car with her cup of coffee, gazing at the Chrysler and Empire State buildings off in the distance. She had talked about wanting to escape. Escape what? I didn't think it was me or Dad. Maybe it was herself? Or maybe it wasn't really that she was leaving, even though that's what it felt like to me; maybe to her it had felt like returning, like coming back or coming home to who she was—"the child Emma," as my aunt had said. I figure that was kind of what my mother had been telling me all the months while she was gone. To become my mother again, she had to find that child she'd lost.

"Well," said Bobby, staring at the cars and trucks streaming across the bridge and the water shimmering below, "I've never lived anywhere else. I can't believe I'm not going to live here anymore."

"Me either." I bit my lower lip.

"Max will miss you."

"I'll miss Max." I scratched him behind the ears and he barked playfully.

"It's been quite a year."

"Yeah," I said.

"You know you can come and visit me in Florida. Anytime."

"Thanks." I figured I probably wouldn't. Who would take me there?

"Doesn't your mother live in Louisiana? That's a lot closer to Florida than Queens."

"She won't always be there," I said, not knowing if that was true, but feeling in my gut that I was right.

"There's e-mail. I bet we meet at races. Competing again. Against each other."

"Or *with* each other," I said.

"A USA team? Together." Bobby knocked his knuckles on mine.

"Who knows?" I smiled as we sat and watched the sun begin to set.

When we got back, it was getting dark, the first star visible in the sky. My father was planting petunias and pansies in a border along the beds in the garden. "Doing your mother's routine," he said, watering them, "in case she comes back soon. I want the place to look nice. Like home. Like she never left."

I got down on my knees to help him dig along the rosebush beds. As I handed him each plant from its black plastic container, he plunked its dense roots downward, adding peat moss and fertilizer. As we churned the earth, something moved on the underside of a crinkled brown leaf. My father turned the leaf over.

"It's a North American tree frog!" I shouted with glee.

"Hmm, how unusual."

"We learned about all kinds of frogs this year in school. They live in the woods, like in the empty lot near our house. They remain frozen all winter. Like a little frogsicle. If you picked one up, you'd think it was a rock, or even dead. But in the spring, they gradually come alive. The first organ to thaw out is its heart."

My father put his arms around me as a full chorus of tree frogs croaked in the nighttime air. We must have looked like two mud pies stuck to each other. "I've learned more from you than you have from me." He held his hand over his heart and swallowed.

One thing I did learn is that the accident changed me and the way I see the world, forever. My mother told me that hope was the last thing in Pandora's box. It will always be the first in mine. I went inside, glued my handprint together, the break still visible. Then I hung it on the wall in the kitchen, out in the open. For everyone to see. Especially me.

Acknowledgments

Thank you from deep in my heart to my brilliant, caring editor, Michelle Frey, who exudes warmth and humor, and her very insightful assistant editor, Michele Burke, for this journey. In addition, thanks to the talented Melissa Nelson, graphic designer, and Sue Warga, the meticulous copy editor. I appreciate the constant support, encouragement, and friendship of my agent, Elizabeth Harding, who stays cheerful through my kvetching. That goes for Steven Zalben as well, particularly at three in the morning over tea. In appreciation to my creative adult children, Alexander and Jonathan, who offer enough material to inspire me for a lifetime; Elizabeth Vardin Newman, for our Wednesday working picnics; and Dr. Ellyn Altman, for showing me the way. I would also like to thank my late swimming and literary buddy, Dr. Bob Boxer, head of pediatric trauma at North Shore

Hospital; Dr. Victor Nannini, oral surgeon; Jan Liebowitz, health teacher; and the Science Museum of Long Island. For their patience with my endless questions, Mary Rita Williams and Bruce Clark, medical malpractice lawyers; Hugh Crowl, astrophysicist; Jennifer Terban, for her tattoo expertise; and my son, Jonathan, who had the same surgery Daniel did as a child. And to the disabled boy with a walker who also had that same operation, and during a school author visit asked me so tentatively, because he couldn't raise his hand, "Can a writer write without writing?" to which I answered, "Yes." And understood. You broke my heart that day.